THE WIDOW MAKER

Led by a vicious hardcase who kills only men, the murderous Widow Gang plunders the rugged wilds of Wyoming Territory. Death, destruction and distraught widows follow in their wake until manhunter Steve Matthews takes up their trail. But he gets far more than he bargained for! Attacked by 'Indians', shadowed by past vendettas and joined by a beautiful Chinese woman, Steve winds up fighting for his own life while struggling to save an entire town from devastation . . .

Books by Lance Howard
in the Linford Western Library:

THE COMANCHE'S GHOST
THE WEST WITCH
THE GALLOWS GHOST

LANCE HOWARD

THE WIDOW MAKER

Complete and Unabridged

LINFORD
Leicester

First ... by

London

First Linford Edition
published 1998
by arrangement with
Robert Hale Limited
London

The right of Howard Hopkins to be identified
as the author of this work has been asserted
by him in accordance with the
Copyright, Designs and Patents Act, 1988

British Library CIP Data

Howard, Lance
    The widow maker.—Large print ed.—
Linford western library
    1. Western stories
    2. Large type books
    I. Title
    823.9'14 [F]

    ISBN 0–7089–5318–2

Published by
F. A. Thorpe (Publishing) Ltd.
Anstey, Leicestershire

Set by Words & Graphics Ltd.
Anstey, Leicestershire
Printed and bound in Great Britain by
T. J. International Ltd., Padstow, Cornwall

This book is printed on acid-free paper

Thanks to Mary Ibekilo for the title
and germ of this story

1

THE Stalwright stage rumbled out of the mountains and into hell.

It clattered and clanked along the winding trail, iron tyres bouncing over rocks and frozen ruts, carriage shuddering, rattling the bones of its passengers. Tom Jenkins took the notion the stage would shake itself apart at any moment. Hell of a thing to happen to a stage hauling as much gold as this one did.

Besides gold, the stage carried four men, two poised in the front seat, snapping the reins and driving over-worked horses north through the treacherous Wyoming wilderness, and two inside, hired guns with attitudes touchy as rattlesnakes and fingers itchier than tinhorns on a losing streak.

With a sharp *crack*! Tom drove the horses harder and glanced at his partner, John Tilton. Drawing a deep breath, he struggled to relax his taut nerves. He wanted no part of this assignment, which was to ride with the stage, its belly full of gold dust, into Wyoming, make a brief stopover at a bank in Deadeye, then drive northward to Montana. Justin Stalwright, who held interests in Deadeye but lived in Montana, owned mines in Colorado and twice yearly ordered shipments transported to a bank in Billings to replenish dwindling monetary assets — which Tom suspected had more to do with the older man's predilection for hurdy-gurdy girls than meeting pay-roll.

Tom spat and let out a disgusted grunt. He felt damned uncomfortable about more than the ride. These shipments struck him as entirely too enticing to bandits on the lookout for an easy stake.

Bandits.

His gaze surveyed the rugged land-scape, studying each minute detail. Trees, Douglas fir and Engelmann pine, dusted with snow that was quickly melting as the day warmed, aspen and cottonwood, leafless, limbs snapping with cold, skirted the left side of the trail, pierced by an ice-blue stream that trickled with brittle-glass voice over rocks. Snow-capped Rockies stabbed gun-metal clouds far in the distance. All thoughts of bandits seemed incongruous, ludicrous. A peaceful late-winter day. Serene. There were no bandits here.

Were there?

What about that Widow Gang?

The thought drove a chill down his spine. He'd heard lots about the rascals lately, a gang run by some fella called the Widow Maker, named as such because he never killed women. Tom uttered a choppy laugh. Perhaps they should have hired women to transport the gold shipment.

The gang had struck all through Colorado and southern Wyoming

Territory over the past half-year-banks, stores, stages. Nothing appeared too big or too small to attract their interest. They'd left a trail of dead men and devastated lonely women.

Rumor claimed the gang consisted of all women, except for the leader. Killer women, vicious as any hardcase fresh from the owlhoot. No one ever got a good look at the rascals, no one who lived to tell the tale, anyway; they always wore masks and eluded the law with a deftness seldom seen since the days of John Barlow.

'What the devil you got on your mind, Tom?' the man next to him asked, brow crinkling.

Tom came from his thoughts, sweat beading on his brow despite the cold. 'What?'

'You ain't worried 'bout bein' held up, are you, Tom? You look white as a ghost'.

Tom shook his head. The man riding beside him was taller by a good four inches, lanky enough to be uncomfortable in the jouncing seat. Knees pulled up to his belly, a Winchester rested across his thighs. John was used to piloting gold runs. This was his fifth, in fact, and he'd never encountered a bit of trouble.

But today Tom swore something crackled in the air, something ominous and disturbing, a trigger to destiny. He couldn't say why he felt that way, only that he did and it set in his mind like a pebble in a boot. He prayed John's sixth run wouldn't prove an unlucky charm.

With the back of his hand Tom wiped sweat from his brow. 'I got a feelin' . . . '

'Pshaw! You an' your fidaddly feelin's! Godamighty, we got the best hired guns money can buy and I'm no slouch with a Winchester myself. Neither are you, Tom. What's to fret on?'

'What about that Widow Gang the papers been talkin' up lately? This is just the sort of thing they'd give a look-see.'

'They got no way of knowin' 'bout this shipment. All the arrangements was made in secret.'

'Men like that got a way of findin' out.' Tom shivered, unable to shake a sudden notion they were being watched. He shot a glance to either side of the trail, spotting nothing suspicious, but that did little to ease his mind.

'Women,' said John.

'Huh?' Tom shook from his thoughts.

'The Widder's Gang's a passel of women. You ain't a-feared of a bunch of women, are you?' John cocked an eyebrow.

Tom frowned. 'You'd be afraid, too, if you had a lick of horse sense! They take orders from that Widow Maker. He ain't called that 'cause he's popular at ladies' socials.'

The other man bellowed a laugh and Tom bristled, embarrassment reddening his cheeks.

A shot ended the conversation.

The report was startling, exaggerated and cracking in the chilly air. The

6

horses bucked and reared, neighing, stuttering in their steps, then plunged ahead in uncontrolled pell-mell terror.

A bullet spanged into the trail ahead, gouging loose a chunk of dirt and ricocheting.

'Christamighty!' blurted John, fighting to hold on to the reins.

Tom struggled with them as well, focusing on the job of steadying the boogered animals instead of his burgeoning panic. The animals refused to stop, though Tom pulled leather with all his might. The stage shuddered, tilted, jerked forward in uneven spurts and bounds.

'What the goddamn hell's goin' on out there?' one of the guns shouted from inside, poking his head out.

The fellow instantly regretted showing himself because another shot cracked and the slug thwacked into the side of the stage, nearly parting his hair.

'Goddammit, someone's a-shootin' at us!' he bellowed, snapping his head inside.

'Didn't 'xactly hire them for brains!' John yelled, pulling the reins with all his strength.

Tom remained silent, concentrating on slowing the rocketing carriage.

You're going to die!

The thought sent a shudder of dread through him and his heart jumped into his throat.

'*Whoa*!' John shouted beside him, but the animals ignored him, thundering onward heedlessly. 'Judas Priest, Tom! We're in a hell of a fix if we can't stop 'em!'

Tom agreed. Ahead the trail grew rockier as it widened and each jounce threatened to send the stage tumbling head over heels.

'Oh Mother of God . . . ' Tom said under his breath.

A volley of gunfire broke out. Bullets burned the air, some whining startlingly close to Tom's head. He swore one tasted the brim of his Stetson.

Riddled with lead, the stage began to come apart, splinters raining, boards

8

shattering. Metal clanged as slugs ricocheted from iron tyres.

A horse stumbled, went down and Tom gave a bleat of terror. The animal had been hit! A crimson gout spouted from its flank. Its hind quarters buckled and the stage, propelled by the panicked flight of the other horses, rammed into the stricken animal.

A sickened sensation filled Tom's belly as the riggings tangled and traces snapped. The horses, terrified beyond limits, slammed to a halt.

The impact lifted the stage's front end clean off the ground and sent the vehicle careening end over end. Tom and John had released the reins and leaped from the seat the instant the horse fell. They landed ten feet away on either side of the trail.

Tom got lucky, landing in a thicket that broke his fall.

John had a similar piece of luck. He came down in the stream with a great splash, hand still cinched about his Winchester.

The stage slammed to a halt with a thunderous crash, exploding into splinters and flying boards. A wheel ripped off, rolling along the trail until it flipped on to its side and wobbled still, thirty feet away. Horses tumbled, one breaking a leg, but the others somehow managing to right themselves in a tangle of riggings.

The hired guns weren't quite as fortunate. One saw the worst coming and endeavored to leap from the stage. He didn't make it. The stage came down on top of him.

The other gun made it no farther than the door; he was trapped in the carriage when it hit. Tom spotted the battered broken body amongst the wreckage.

Tom gave the situation little thought. He was too concerned for his own life. He struggled to his feet, drawing his six-shooter. Shooting a glance at the stream, he saw John splashing his way out.

'Hey, we gotta — ' Tom started.

A shot stopped him short.

John took a sudden skip backwards, a chunk of his forehead turning to pulp. He went down in a splash and Tom watched his partner's body begin to drift downstream.

In nearly the same instant, Tom dived, not knowing what sixth sense warned him, but damn thankful it had.

Lead flew, digging up chunks of earth and chipping bark from trees. Most of the bullets punched into the ground where he had stood not a moment before.

Hitting the ground, he rolled, keeping his gun close to his chest. He came to his feet and ran for the cover of a huge cottonwood at stream's edge. Heart thundering, his pulse throbbed in his throat.

He chanced a look from behind the tree. The woodland had gone deathly still and he saw nothing. The horses, spooked, tangled in their riggings and broken traces, neighed and stamped, unable to flee. Two of the animals lay still. But that was all.

Tom pressed his back against the tree and closed his eyes, calculating his chances of escaping the gang he knew was hidden behind the boulders and brush. None. Zero. *Nada* or any other damn way you sliced it. He'd be dead before he made it five feet.

'You can have the gold!' he suddenly yelled in desperation. 'It's yours! Take it! Please, just let me live.' He tried to swallow his heart.

A laugh floated across the crisp air. A woman's laugh. Cold, cruel, mocking. 'We're gonna take it anyhow, mister! You got no choice!'

A rush of movement caught his attention and he chanced a look. Seven figures dashed from the cover of trees and boulders and brush; two who lay flat on the ground leaped up. They materialized like wraiths, taking a zigzagging course towards him, presenting difficult targets. They knew he'd never hit them all, unlikely even one. A brazen lot.

By their builds he saw they were all women! Except for the one in front, a husky fellow with one eye. None wore masks and that made him shudder. They counted on leaving no witnesses.

With the charge, all his suspicions were confirmed: the Widow Gang had hit the stage!

Tom made a split-second decision. His last act would be one of dignity. He'd never get them all but one would stop a bullet and that would be the leader.

Gripping his courage, he stepped from behind the tree and raised his gun.

Something hit him. He neither saw it coming nor fathomed what it was. It sailed through the air, tangled itself about his neck, choking him. Reflexively he triggered a shot before dropping his gun and prying at the thing circling his throat. It was some sort of cord and ball arrangement.

A bolas! He fought to loosen the constricting bands, stumbling, gasping.

Distantly, he heard a yell. He'd gotten lucky: his shot had not been in vain. The outlaw leader grabbed at the sudden flower of blood blossoming at his shoulder, uttering a string of curses.

Tom's satisfaction was short-lived. Shots blasted and white-hot lead pierced his body. He stopped four bullets, any one of them enough to kill him. His legs buckled and more bullets tore into him before he hit the ground. But it no longer mattered because suddenly he felt no pain and saw no light.

★ ★ ★

'Jesus H., Brace!' snapped Shale, as she examined the leader's shoulder wound. She frowned and made a grimace that made it plain she had no teeth. The last of her choppers had rotted out two years ago and Brace Carrigan reckoned the leathery woman wore it like a

14

badge. A percentage had been knocked out in fights with men, most of whom wound up on the short end of the stick; disease had claimed the rest.

Brace peered at his second and spat. His eye held her gaze. 'Goddamn little weasel got off a lucky shot, is all.' Disgust punctuated his raspy voice. 'Bullet's still in there, I can feel it.'

Shale's brow crinkled and she shook her head. Her skin looked as worn and wrinkled as an old saddle and her brown hair, streaked with grey and washed as often as the stage drove north, was stuffed beneath a battered Stetson. 'Gotta come out, Brace, no two ways about it.'

Brace's one eye narrowed, fury and disgust turning his thin lips. He had a stocky build, muscled like a longhorn. A straggly beard touched his collar bone and greasy strands of brown hair snaked from beneath his hat. He had an angular face and hollow cheeks and a nose repeatedly broken. One eye was sewn shut: he'd lost it in a fight, compliments of another man's Bowie. That man had lost more than an orb by the time Brace punched his ticket. He reckoned his head still decorated an El Pueblo saloon.

'First we get that gold.' He motioned and around him five women besides Shale set about extracting the gold pouches from the crashed stage. One of the women, a gal named Bertha, who weighed half again more than Brace and was poison to the eyes, gave the dead gun a lusty kick and uttered a sadistic giggle.

'Swear you enjoy your work too much,' said Calamity Annie, a wisp of a girl. Frail-looking with mousy hair and wire spectacles, she was hell with a gun. A dime novel about Wild Bill Hickok was tucked in her belt.

Bertha spat and made a face that resembled a lumpy Jack-o-lantern. 'Hell, 'cept for Brace never did meet a man I could stand more than a few minutes in the hay.' She kicked the guard again for good measure.

The remaining members, Mex triplets with black hair and piercing brown eyes, scurried about the wreckage, collecting sacks. One stepped over to the dead driver and retrieved her bolas, securing it to her belt. All had angelic faces violated by devil eyes and all wielded expert bolas and long-bladed knives. Their mother had named them April, May and June after the peaceful, gentle months, but peace and gentleness seldom applied to the three.

After collecting the gold, they scurried into the hills and retrieved their horses. Bertha fetched Brace's sorrel while the leader kept watch on the gold. They stashed the pouches into saddle-bags and mounted.

Shale gave a sadistic chuckle as she stepped into the saddle. 'Best we get you to a sawbones, Brace, 'fore you go belly-up on us. What the hell would we do without you?' A wry grin turned her lips.

Brace cast her a glare strong enough to corrode silver. 'Best you don't get no ideas on findin' out.'

Her toothless grin widened. 'Hell, I'm just joshin', Brace.'

'I ain't in a joshin' mood.' He climbed into the saddle, wincing, blood streaming from the wound. Sweat beaded on his brow and he felt the weakness creeping in. If he didn't have the wound tended to soon the driver's lucky shot would make the history books.

★ ★ ★

Doctor Jason Parker peered out the window of his office at the bright day, wondering if there could be a prettier morning or happier man in the entire West. The sun coated the field with honey and sparkled from patches of snow and diamond crystals of ice. Tree branches glistened and everything looked bright and new. While not an old man, neither was he young and he reckoned he had waited a long time to find the happiness he held now.

He'd passed forty summers on this earth, but felt half that since Sarah came along. Grey touched the edges of his hair and mutton chop sideburns. Handsome in a comfortable sort of way, he was neither a dandy nor one of the rugged hardy types prevalent in Deadeye. Somewhere in-between and that pleased him just fine.

Originally from San Francisco, he had only recently relocated his practice to Wyoming, despite protests from his family — a brother and sister — and a lack of monetary assets. Lack of funds was part of the problem: he'd spent nearly all his savings buying Sarah's freedom from her Chinese master, but how could he not? He loved her more deeply than he'd ever loved anything and no amount of money compared to that.

Sarah loved him as well, though a good ten years his junior and barely able to speak a word of English when he met her in the Chinatown laundry. He'd observed her for months, snatching small gems of time in which he could be with her until the day came when he confronted her master, fashioning some lie about needing a reliable slave for his practice. Reluctantly, her owner had parted with his slave for $1,000, an exorbitant sum but one he knew Jason would pay. He offered Sarah immediate freedom but she returned home with him and stayed. They had never married, creating no little amount of scandal and wagging tongues, but he didn't give a damn. Together they worked to rebuild his practice in the wilds of Wyoming, far away from the world she despised, the world of a sweat-soaked and opium-clouded San Francisco slave laundry, where she was forced to labor sixteen or more hours a day over scalding steam and boiling water, with blistering chemicals and soaps and live in filthy roach-and-rodent-infested rooms crammed with other slaves. Girls were commonly hopped up with suspectly pure opium and presented to white men eager for

20

young Orientals and unburdened by morals or compassion.

Hearing soft footfalls behind him, he turned.

'Sarah, my darling, you're back.' A gentleness softened his face as he saw her standing in the doorway.

The girl smiled, delicate Asian features aglow with the sunlight that filtered through the window. Warmth shone in her eyes, darkly rich, flavored with the secrets of the Orient. The scent of jasmine touched his nostrils.

'I have the herbs,' she said in a soft voice, only a hint of an accent detectable. He marveled at how hard she had worked to speak English fluently; she probably knew the technicalities of language better than he. Sarah went to the desk where she took care of the appointment book and ledgers — she'd taught herself to read and write and it always amazed him how rapidly she absorbed knowledge, craved it — set a basket of flowers and foliage atop the blotter.

21

A Chinese gown, embroidered with a poppy and gold pattern, shimmered with sunlight as she went to a cabinet and selected empty bottles labeled with the names of the various herbs she collected in the woods near the house. Later she would boil and crush the herbs and flowers into teas and powders, each with its particular healing power, then place them in the bottles, Chinese remedies, potions most western doctors refused to put stock in. But he did, trusting her knowledge of herbs as much as she trusted his of modern medicine. He had learned the subtle curatives of herbal teas and acupuncture and she had studied the workings of sterile cloths and permanganate of potash, vitriol and carbolic.

He examined the herbs, smiling. 'These'll do just fine, Sarah. We should have plenty, now.'

She said nothing and he turned to see her gaze fixed on some distant spot beyond the window. Her small body went rigid as she stared, finally looking at him. He saw worry in her dark eyes.

'There is a storm approaching.' Her voice remained soft but something in it gave him chill.

'Nonsense, Sarah, the day's crystal clear. It couldn't be more beautiful and calm.'

A sound reached his ears then: hoofbeats. He wondered if that was what she had meant.

'It's only a patient or someone from town.' His voice lost a touch of its lightness as something vaguely disturbing swept through him.

'There are no appointments and he wears a mask. Do not let him in.'

He went to the window and looked out to see a man rein to a halt. A mask covered the rider's lower face, and vague dread became a tingle of apprehension. His gaze settled on the man's shoulder; it was soaked with blood.

'Do not let him in,' Sarah repeated,

voice more emphatic, tinged with fear.

'Nonsense, Sarah. I'm a doctor. That man's hurt. I have to treat him.'

'He is a bandit.' She moved away and pretended to work with the basket of herbs. He'd grown used to her moodiness and while he could never figure it out he reckoned it resulted from her experiences bending to the domination of another.

Jason frowned, resignation in his eyes. 'He may be an outlaw, but he's hurt. I took an oath to preserve life, no matter whose. I have no choice.'

An urgent banging rattled the front door. His heart quickened. He wondered if he should listen to Sarah, knowing her intuition was far more accurate than his in such matters. Right or wrong it made little difference. He would do what his conscience dictated.

'Please, go let him in while I wash my hands.'

'I will not.' Her almond eyes narrowed and her face set with determination. She would not be argued with and he knew it. It irked him but he could do nothing about it but accept it as part of her nature, along with the good and gentle things he loved. He blew out an exasperated sigh and left the room, going to the front door.

A man stood in the doorway, a man who gave him the feeling he got upon seeing a masked hangman standing at the lever of a gallows. A blocky man, with one eye and a mask covering his lower face, and a gushing shoulder. Blood dripped on to the porch.

'You the sawbones?' Voice raspy, commanding, a man used to being obeyed. The fellow's eye settled on him and he suppressed the urge to shudder.

'Yes, I'm Doc Parker.'

'Got me a little hole in my shoulder, Doc. Bullet's still in there. You're gonna get it out.' Ordering tone, almost mocking. Jason detested it but kept any look of such off his face as the man's hand slid over the butt of the revolver in the holster at his hip to emphasize his 'request'.

He stepped aside. 'Come in, then. We'll take a look.'

He guided the man into the office and pointed to the examination table, indicating for him to sit. He noticed the man giving Sarah a look he didn't care for, not exactly lust, something stranger, something unreadable. It was almost . . . what? Pity? No, that couldn't be. Why would a hardcase pity Sarah? It made no sense. Doc Parker shook off the thought and busied himself with pulling the sterile instruments Sarah had boiled from a bag and placing them on a tray, which he rolled over to the table. He peered at the man's shoulder. A bloody mess.

'What happened?' He knew the man would likely lie but asked just the same.

'Don't ask questions you don't want answered, Doc.' Coldness iced his tone. Jason felt the urge to back away from the man, as if intimidated by the fellow's very presence.

He nodded, licking his lips. 'All

right, but that's a serious wound. I'm going to cut away some of the shirt and clean it first.'

The hardcase nodded. 'Do what it takes, Doc. And don't take your time with it; I'm in a hurry.'

Jason's brow crinkled and he reached for a pair of scissors, first throwing a glance at Sarah. Dragons of worry breathed flame behind her brown eyes. Despite her objections, she came over to assist. She did not like the situation, but would be at his side; she always was.

Prying up the bloody fabric, he clipped away the shirt, careful not to nick open flesh. Bright blood soaked the material but around the edges it was turning brown. In places the shirt was stuck to the wound. He jerked it loose and the man winced but made no sound.

Cutting completed, he examined the wound, probing its ragged borders. Fresh blood bubbled out and Jason cleansed the wound with carbolic and boiled cotton pads, wiping away blood and bacteria. The hole was ugly but he'd seen worse.

'Peacemaker?' the Doc asked, having seen enough wounds caused by the weapon of choice in these parts.

The man nodded. 'Reckon it don't matter that you know.' Jason didn't care for the way the man said it.

'The bullet has to come out.'

'Take it out and don't be delicate about it. I ain't the squeamish sort.'

Jason sighed. 'No, I don't imagine you are.'

He lifted the scalpel from the tray, light glinting from shiny metal and reflecting in the outlaw's eye. 'Wouldn't you rather lie down — '

'Just take it out, Doc. I ain't the patient sort, either.'

Jason licked his lips. 'Whiskey?'

The man nodded and Jason handed him a flat flask he always kept on the tray for such operations. The man pulled down the mask and suddenly Jason knew he'd just made a terrible mistake in his effort to be kind to the fellow and save him some pain. He now knew the man's face, the race of death. Heart pounding, he glanced at Sarah, who, from the tense flutter of her eyes, realised it as well. He swallowed, fighting not to think about it.

The man took a gulp of whiskey and set the bottle down, an expression oddly like a smile on his lips, but not quite, an expression of evil and devils, had Jason believed in such things. He glanced at the scalpel in his hand; he could be rough, inflict so much pain the man would black out. Then they could tie him up and he could take out the bullet while Sarah fetched the marshal.

His hand moved towards the outlaw and he didn't know whether it trembled slightly or whether the outlaw simply read something in his eyes. The outlaw's hand darted up, clamping about Jason's wrist and stopping the scalpel.

'Don't make any mistakes, Doc,' he

29

said, face hard. 'I don't like mistakes.'

Jason nodded and the man released his hand.

He slid the scalpel into the soft folds of flesh and muscle, probing for the bullet. He located the slug, which relieved him more than he cared to admit, suddenly having no desire to cause this man any more discomfort than necessary.

The bullet came out with a gentle upward sweep of the scalpel. With a clink, he dropped it into a steel basin on the table. The man took another swig of the whiskey.

Jason cleaned the wound a second time and set a plaster and sterile cotton wraps to it.

Finishing, he eyed the man. 'Doubt you'll have to worry about infection, but there's always a chance so you best take it slow for a while. I'd suggest bed rest.'

The man laughed; it was an unpleasant sound. 'Much obliged, Doc, but I ain't got that option.'

He slid off the table while Jason went to a cabinet and pulled a bottle from the shelf.

'Laudanum?' the man said.

'You'll need it. That'll hurt like a sonofabitch for a few days.' He handed it to the outlaw.

'Reckon this is on the house . . . ' The outlaw peered at him, eye as empty as a deadman's.

Frozen by the stare, Jason didn't move but from the corner of his eye saw Sarah flash him a look, telling him to agree to whatever the man said, a point he had no inclination to argue. 'Reckon it is.'

The man took a few steps towards the door, stopped, turned, giving Sarah a look that again spoke of pity. Yes, pity, he felt sure of it this time. The outlaw's one-eyed gaze shifted to Jason, who felt another chill shudder along his spine.

The shot came suddenly and without warning. The man's hand swept in a blur of movement for the Schofield at his hip. The gun cleared leather and belched a snap of flame and blue smoke. Sarah screamed, a prolonged wail of utter terror and wrenching loss.

The bullet punched into Jason's chest, sending him backwards over the tray of instruments. They scattered across the floor, glinting sunlight.

He lay on the floor, blood pumping from a gaping wound in his chest. He struggled to utter a few words, tell Sarah he loved her, but they came out a gurgle.

Tears rushing down her face, Sarah rushed to his side, drawing him close, holding him, he knew, for the last time. He saw death, his death, reflected in her tear-glossed eyes.

Sarah looked up at the bandit, hate in her dark eyes.

He leveled the gun at her and she screamed, 'Kill me! Kill me, too!'

He laughed, the look of pity returning. 'Don't worry, ma'am. I won't kill you. Don't kill women. I saw my daddy kill my ma, then I killed him. I've been killin' him ever since.' The man holstered his gun and backed out of the room.

In the distance, Jason heard receding hoofbeats, muffled, fading and even Sarah's gentle sobbing grew faint. He felt her kiss his dry lips, then nothing more.

2

STEVE MATTHEWS drew a deep breath of morning air and smiled, despite the seriousness of the job at hand. Riding the trail at an even pace, he began whistling some tune he'd heard in a saloon in Cheyenne.

The autumn morning was glorious, radiant. Leaves painted in brilliant shades of gold, orange and red sparkled with frost that quickly turned to dew as the brassy sun climbed higher in a crystal-blue sky

While wondrous and peace-inspiring, the vista made him feel somehow insignificant and humbled. Wyoming Territory, whose name was derived from the Delaware Indian term 'at the big plains', was another world to him, staggering in its vastness and diverse palette. Part of the Louisiana

Purchase in 1803 the land boasted varied terrain, two-thirds rolling plain and about one-third Rocky Mountains. Veined with rivers and streams, laden with game and natural resource, it had been forged by fur trappers in the early 1800s. The fur trade declined after 1840 and the provisioning of westward-bound travelers — via numerous trails such as the Oregon and Mormon — became the primary activity. When the Union Pacific Railroad punched through between '67 and '69, it stimulated ranching and mining. It was far removed from the dusty, never-changing landscape of Matadero, Texas, the town he hailed from. Something about this corner of the West aroused his Indian blood, Apache on his mother's side.

A ghost smile haunted his lips. He could easily adjust to the rugged idyllic life this territory had to offer. Elana would feel the same, he felt sure of it. When he reached his destination he would wire her, describe the wonders he had seen, convince her they should stake a claim and move here after they married.

As soon as he finished this last case, their new life could begin. He saw a future filled with promise, happiness and it pleased him no end. He couldn't imagine anything interfering with it.

He drew up, taking another long breath and leaning his forearms against the saddle horn.

Retirement. He hadn't given it much thought until now, but he had made her a promise and he would keep it. For Steve Matthews was a bounty hunter, a man hired to chase down hardcases the law couldn't or wouldn't deal with and bring them to justice at the end of a rope or by hot lead. For the most part he felt comfortable in that role. It provided him a sense of worth, knowing he was helping folks who felt powerless against such men.

He'd been a bounty hunter for only a short while, no more than two years, before that a deputy in Matadero, but it would soon come to an end. He would give it up with little sense of loss or regret. Life held more important things, such as his impending marriage to Elana, and man-hunting could be damned dangerous business — no business for a married man, so before leaving he promised her this would be his last case.

Of course, he neglected to tell her what the case involved. If he had, she would have fretted endlessly or argued him out of going.

For his last assignment was easily his most dangerous:

Bring down a gang. Not just any gang, but one that brandished fear and death as weapons, leaving a trail of dead men and carnage, destruction and weeping widows. A gang composed of six women and one man. While the notion of an all-women gang might have struck him as comical under different circumstances, their track record struck him as anything but. Killing, robbing, maiming, they had devastated towns spanning an area stretching from Colorado to Montana. The leader, an unknown hardcase simply known as the Widow Maker — many a lonely woman could attest to how the hardcase came by his handle — showed no mercy or restraint in his wanton ravages.

Odd thing about the hombre, though: he never killed women. Steve wondered about that. He'd never seen the likes of such in the two years he'd been manhunting.

The gang wore masks, so their faces remained a mystery, but some soul had attested to the fact the leader had only one eye. That, if accurate, made things easier. A one-eyed outlaw shouldn't prove hard to spot. Proof was another matter. Masked men — or women in this case — couldn't be identified and were best caught in the act. But Steve wasn't overly concerned with that matter. When he found this man he'd likely not have the luxury of bringing him to justice pronounced by any court. Men like that didn't usually come peaceably. The only justice for this type of hardcase was decreed by Judge Six-gun.

Now the gals, they were a different story. A gang of women, all as ruthless as the leader himself, perhaps more so. Reports on them were vague, given to superficial descriptions with a healthy measure of windy thrown in. From what he could glean, one was a large blocky woman and one was small and fraillooking. Three appeared to have relatively the same builds and looks; accounts held they were sisters. Another, who appeared to be the leader's second, was nondescript.

Steve lifted his hat and mopped sweat from his brow. He'd been in the saddle for a good four hours and his bones ached. Guiding the bay left, he dismounted and tethered to a cottonwood branch. He went to the stream and knelt, peering at his reflection in a pool of water. His skin color and looks fell between white and red; a coppery tan, more the result of days riding under the hot sun than his Apache heritage, shaded his skin and his dark eyes looked bright and alive. Starry-eyed, some called him and he was forced to agree. He viewed the world as growing, expanding, full of potential and promise. When man learned to get along, work together, all would prosper. He could see that world, that gleaming future time, hope for it, though others, the narrow-minded the short-sighted, could not. Blemishes created by outlaws such as the Widow Gang could be scrubbed from the face of the world and never missed. Elana said he chased windmills like that fella from some tale she'd told him about. Perhaps she was right, but he hoped he never changed. Some windmills needed to be chased.

He splashed water into his face; it was chilled, refreshing. Wiping off with his bandanna he stood, stretching, limbs stiff, tailbone aching.

Not much farther. Last reports put

the gang in the vicinity of southern Wyoming Territory. Hired by the wife of a man the gang had killed, a guard or something on a stage carrying a shipment of gold dust, he'd sent wires to a friend of his who worked for the Rangers. His friend had informed him of the robbery, which had occurred seven months ago. The trail might prove cold, but it gave him a starting point. The faster he tied up this case the faster he returned to Elana and started a new life. Their life.

Making his way back to his horse, he chuckled, feeling at peace. He had planned it all while riding the trail, their life together. What he knew about cattle he would combine with the money he'd saved from his last few jobs, enough to outfit a small spread, purchase some beeves. With bank help he would build a home complete with gravity pipes and all the amenities; that would convince Elana it wasn't a pipe dream, another windmill.

A sound snapped him from his

reverie and he looked up to see a black bird alight on a cottonwood branch. A crow. Eyes narrowing, he stared at the bird, a vague sense of premonition stirring his Apache soul, but he passed it off as nothing. Odd, that bird; it seemed to have followed him since he reached Wyoming. Everywhere he turned there it was, peering at him with glassy black eyes, cawing as if it had some great tale to tell. His Indian side saw it as a good omen, a spirit guide to bring him through this case.

The bird squawked and he laughed. 'Fly, my friend,' he said, lifting his hat and arching a hand above his brow to shield his eyes from the sun. 'Fly and guide me. She's a-waitin' on me back home.'

With a thin smile, he shook his head and went back to his bay. He stroked the horse's neck, then stepped into the saddle, breathing deeply of the fragrant scent of fall leaves, feeling a warmth glow in his being that told him everything would go the way he wanted it to.

He was wrong.

Dead wrong.

Guiding his horse back on to the trail, he surveyed the surroundings ahead. To his right the land rose at a steep angle, rock-strewn, littered with scrub brush and stunted trees. The trail itself was rutted and dry, blanketed by dead leaves.

Above him the crow gave a chuckling caw and he looked up, seeing it glide at an angle into the wood-land. The sense of premonition grew stronger, darker. A warning.

Something felt wrong.

As he edged the horse forward, he mulled over the feeling, amazed anything that foreboding could intrude on such serenity. He rarely experienced those feelings these days. As a child, more Apache than white, they nagged him frequently, but with age they grew distant, retreating behind the practical common sense side of him that took over. Usually it indicated some impending encounter with a particular hardcase he had tracked down.

But what did it mean this time?

He felt sure the Widow Gang could be nowhere near. At least he hoped that wasn't the case because he was ill prepared to encounter them at this junture. He planned on enlisting local law when he found a lead to their whereabouts, form a posse. He wanted no part of seven armed bandits on his own.

He slowed a notch, scanning the area for a sign of anything wrong.

Nothing.

His brow crinkled. He spotted nothing off kilter, yet something in his Apache blood tingled, made his heart beat faster and sent a prickle of warning through the hairs on the back of his neck.

The crow swooped and circled, cawed. The bird felt it, too, he reckoned; animals perceived things humans did not. White men never listened to animals; perhaps that was their greatest folly. Apache did and Steve Matthews listened, now. He listened with an intensity that possessed him when he knew danger drew close. Elana accused him of being too blasé about his work, of not showing a lick of sense when it came to life-threatening situations, but he knew different. Despite his rose-colored outlook and sometimes purile way of seeing the world, he was anything but reckless. Any manhunter who was didn't survive long in this line of work. Elana had never understood that; that's why she worried herself unduly. He could have told her how his senses became alive, hyper-sensitive when danger threatened, aware of subtleties and unseen details, the scent of evil. He could have told her but she wouldn't have listened. She was not Apache.

He eyed the circling crow, hoping to get an idea from which direction the threat came, what it was.

The first thing that occurred to him was the possibility of some predatory animal stalking him. Bear, mountain cat, wolf; any one of them was likely, so he slid his Winchester from its saddleboot, eyes roving left and right, searching for any hint of movement.

His gaze stopped and he tensed as sound caught his ears.

Mountain lion?

No, it was no cat, he realized, but the revelation came too late. The sound came above and to the right — a horse snorting. He twisted, gaze sweeping up.

A flash of movement and a whoop rang out, jangling the silence. Shock went through him but he had no time to react, for riders appeared at the top of the rise.

He had expected predators, animal or human.

But he had not expected Indians!

The sudden appearance of five Indian braves sent a chill down his back. Gussied up with war paint and well-outfitted with fast horses and plentiful weapons — bows, lances, shields — they postured for attack. He took them in at a glance, something striking him suddenly peculiar about the brood, though he couldn't pinpoint what.

He had no time to dwell on the notion. With urgency he sent his bay skittering left, aiming for the protective cover of the trees.

He didn't make it.

An arrow buried itself in his shoulder. Pain burned sharp, sudden, and the impact kicked him out of the saddle.

He slammed into the ground, crashing down on the injured shoulder. The air exploded from his lungs and his head reeled. Pain lanced his shoulder.

By all accounts he should have died in the next moment. Stunned, wounded, he made easy prey for the Indians manoeuvering their horses down the slope, whooping.

The only thing that saved him was his horse, who was between him and the attackers, rearing in fright and neighing in terror. By the time the horse bolted Steve's senses had returned and he realized he had retained his hold on his rifle.

He sprang to his feet and ran for the cover of a huge cottonwood, levering shells into the chamber of his Winchester and pumping shots that struck empty ground.

Arrows ploughed into the soil, chasing his heels, barely missing.

He reached the tree and pressed his back to it, gasping. Sweat poured down his face. The arrow stuck out of his shoulder, hurting like the devil. Pain radiated to his fingertips as each breath jostled the shaft. He set the rifle against the tree and peered at the wound, which pumped blood. Bracing himself and gritting his teeth, he gripped the shaft. He couldn't pull it out; to do so would tear half the meat from his shoulder. He knew too well what Indian arrowheads could do to a man's hide.

Having no other choice, he snapped off the shaft, leaving the arrowhead embedded in his flesh. Pain stabbed his shoulder, bringing tears to his eyes. Blood bubbled out around the wound, soaking his shirt, staining his coat, but the flow wasn't fast or life-threatening.

Forcing back the pain, he snatched up the Winchester and chanced a look. The Indians had disappeared but he felt their presence. He spotted their horses bunched a hundred yards south, caught faint rustlings in the brush, saw hints of movement near a boulder. Again the thought of something off kilter struck him. Indians usually hid themselves better than that. Something else: their mounts were geared more like a white man's.

He quickly put it out of his mind. The more immediate problem of getting out of this alive demanded his attention. Outnumbered and out-weaponed, he was at a serious disadvantage. His horse had bolted with his supplies, including spare bullets. All he had were the shells in his Winchester and five bullets in the Peacemaker at his hip, a sixth in his coat pocket. Enough for five Indians, had they been sitting in a row waiting for him to pluck them off.

The attackers were probably Arapaho, though by all accounts they hadn't attacked any white men in his area for some time. Most Indians resided on reservations, now, except for a few renegades, which he reckoned these must be.

An arrow ploughed into the ground beside the tree and he started. They knew where he was. Likely they would try to manoeuver around him, cut off all retreat.

Sweat trickled down his face and his heart hammered behind his ribs. He needed to think of something quick. Perhaps if he could take out one or two of the attackers, even the odds a bit, the rest would retreat. He chanced another look, bringing up the Winchester.

A scurry of movement; he spotted a brave to his left, angling around to the side and raising a bow.

Steve didn't hesitate. He jerked the trigger. The Indian squealed and stopped in his tracks, a bloody hole in his side.

The Indian's move surprised Steve almost as much as the attack. Most Indians weren't that sloppy.

Taking advantage of Steve's hesitation, the fellow stumbled for cover behind a tree before he could squeeze off another shot. He fired all the same; lead ricocheted from the tree, chipping bark.

A round of arrows followed his shot, each thunking into the tree or ploughing into the ground. He jerked back as one shaved leaves from a branch just above his head. He counted to five and spun, firing three quick shots in the general direction from which the arrows had come. Lead spanged from boulders, chipping slivers of rock.

Catching a hint of movement, he fired at a patch of brush. An unIndian-like curse rang out. Odd, but many

51

reservation Indians had picked up colorful language from the white man.

The Indian who had cursed bolted from cover, running towards a boulder. Steve got another shock, then. The Indian abandoned his quiver in favor of a Smith & Wesson. He sent three bullets in Steve's direction. Lead gouged chunks of bark from the tree and Steve withdrew his head, cussing.

Arapahos with revolvers. That made matters all the worse. If they were all heeled, he didn't have much of a chance.

His gaze darted left and right, seeking a path of retreat. Chances of getting out of this alive looked slimmer by the moment. One Indian was down, wounded, but that left four to contend with.

Steve levered a shell into the chamber and triggered a shot, darting sideways in the same move.

An Indian scampered from behind a boulder, blasting away with a revolver and with sinking dread Steve knew they all carried firearms. The bullets missed but the Arapaho seemed much more comfortable with the guns than their traditional Indian weaponry.

Steve reached the shelter of a boulder. The attackers had not managed to circle him so far, in fact, they seemed amazingly inept at stealth and native warfare. Whatever the reason behind it, it provided him with his only chance.

Crouching, he brought up the Winchester and fired at the last position of the Indian brandishing the Smith & Wesson. The rifle's kick made his shoulder throb.

A shout of anguish rang out and he knew he had scored another hit, probably only superficial or the fellow wouldn't be screaming so loud.

Another shock: the Indians did the unthinkable — they ran!

Four of them sprinted for their horses, jumping on to the mounts and reining around. Amazed, he merely watched, forgetting to shoot.

One of the wounded men, arm

dangling limp at his side, made his horse and climbed into the saddle. The other, gut shot, reached his horse but failed in two attempts to gain his mount. He fell to the ground and his companions cast him a swift look, then gigged their horses into motion, deserting the wounded man.

Steve blew out an amazed sigh. Wasn't like Indians to leave one of their own, wasn't even like a white man, unless they were hardcases . . .

Hardcases?

Steve pushed the thought away and edged from behind the boulder, relief overtaking his surprise. He angled towards the fallen man, wanting a better look at the fellow and possibly to secure the horse. The brave suddenly blasted away with his Smith & Wesson and Steve dived sideways. He hadn't expected the fellow, wounded as bad as he was, to be quite so itchy on the trigger.

Steve mulled it over. He had no idea how much ammunition the man carried and it wasn't in his nature to shoot at a stationary target. He would have to leave the fellow, who might eventually gain his horse but likely die in the saddle — if he didn't, he'd die where he lay. The wound looked serious; most likely the bullet had punctured an intestine. That meant peritonitis and certain doom.

Steve retreated, keeping out of sight and angling south along the trail's edge. His own wound while not life-threatening, if treated immediately, would become so in a short spell. He had no horse and couldn't get close enough to the Indian's mount without stopping lead. Deadeye lay at least thirty miles away in his estimation, but he had little choice: he would have to walk it.

3

IT was going to be a hell of a walk.

The sun glared high overhead, turning the October day unusually warm. Sweat trickled down Steve's face, chest, and his heart beat thickly. His outlook on Wyoming terrain had darkened considerably. Now all he saw was rough, uneven ground, strewn with rocks and jutting roots, patches of thorn brush that tore at his britches and raked his flesh. Bugs, drawn by his blood and sweat, nettled him, buzzing incessantly, biting.

His wound throbbed with a deep burning ache that at times nearly brought tears to his eyes. He swore he felt the arrowhead grinding against bone with each step taken.

He stumbled to the stream, dropping to his knees and scooping up a handful of water, drinking it, then splashing more into his face. His throat burned and his tongue felt thick, lips gummy. The danger of fever grew more likely with every mile. Already he was sweating copiously, certainly more than the walk warranted. He glanced at the wound, fingers going to the brown-caked edges. If his whiskey supply hadn't run off with his horse, he could have doused the wound, lessened the chance of infection. It needed medical attention soon. It wouldn't take green-bellied blowflies and soft white maggots long to infest the open flesh.

He'd made slow progress. The going had been tough, treacherous at points. He had stumbled often, fallen and skinned his knuckles and scraped flesh from his palms, only to push himself back to his feet and resume his arduous course with single-minded determination. Three miles had trickled away. That wasn't a good pace and rest was out of the question. With each step he felt an overpowering desire to stop, lay himself on a bed of leaves and sleep. But he couldn't. He needed as much distance between him and the Indians before darkfall as possible.

He had managed to retain his grip on his rifle, but it felt heavy as lead in his hand, a hindrance but a necessary one. He dared not drop it, even with the Peacemaker at his hip. Too many dangers lurked in the woodland.

He stared into the water, his haggard reflection peering back. If Elana ever saw him in this condition she'd never let him out alone again. Her worst fears had come true, though not in a way either of them would have expected. He would not be bested by some outlaw, nor even the Indians. By some strange quirk of fate, it would be nature that brought him down. Because if he didn't make town soon, he would die here in the woods and it was damned unlikely anyone would ever find his body.

Gritting his teeth, he forced himself to his feet and peered at the trail ahead, then stumbled onward, forcing himself not to think of the pain in his shoulder and the hunger gnawing at his belly.

Those Indians. Why had they deserted the attack? They weren't hurt that bad and carried guns. They could have finished him. Something about that attack struck him as peculiar, puzzling. What reason did they have to attack one man traveling south? He posed no threat to them; hell, he was Indian himself. How had they happened on him in the first place? Few knew he was in Wyoming, except for Elana, the woman who'd hired him, a handful of other folks in Matadero. Certainly no Indians knew, nor should they have cared. He was here to track an outlaw gang; they would have no interest in that.

A chance attack? Had renegade Indians merely stumbled on to him and decided to take advantage of their luck? Perhaps, but that struck him as unlikely. They were geared for war and Deadeye was thirty miles from where the attack occurred; they certainly couldn't have had it in mind to attack the town. So what would they be doing waiting along an infrequently ridden trail? It was almost as if they had expected him to come.

A stab of pain at his shoulder jarred him from his thoughts and he gasped, clenching his teeth against it.

The ground jittered before his vision and ahead trees and brush looked strangely foreign, tinged with a haze that distorted tree limbs into reaching arms, turned brown leaves bloody. A breeze whisked through the leaves, making a shushing, whispering sound, sending some drizzling to the ground. The stream murmured like voices of the dead, beckoning him to join them.

An hallucination, frightening. He blinked and it vanished. Relief flooded him, but only briefly. His condition was worsening, fever rising.

Above, the crow alighted on a cottonwood branch, cawing loudly. He cursed at the bird, at himself.

The sun skipped higher, at once directly overhead, then suddenly dipping towards the distant mountains.

The day darkened and shadows thickened, looking grotesque and strangely alive as they stretched from trees and boulders and brush.

Another mile.

An endless mile, each step fought for and won, but at a cost. His strength was fading, will dissolving. He forced all thoughts of failure from his mind, determined to return to Elana, his beautiful Elana, and marry her.

At times he glimpsed her face, smiling, drawing him along, giving him purpose and hope. Another hallucination, but one that steadied his resolve.

The sun dipped closer to the slate mountain tops, splashing them with ochre then blood-red.

The woodland turned gloomy and shadows blackened.

A sound. A scampering to his left. Startling, but merely some creature of the forest scurrying for cover as he trampled by.

A snake slithered across the path and he halted, nearly stumbling over it. The last thing he needed was be to be snake bit. He had no idea what poisonous snakes Wyoming held but had no particular desire to find out.

The crow squawked and he looked up to see it swoop from a branch and circle overhead. An ominous sense of danger tingled deep inside, warning him.

'I'll listen . . . ' he mumbled, halting, ears pricked for the slightest sound.

Had the Indians come back?

No, not this time. It was something else, some other threat.

A hint of movement to his right —

The cat sprang out of nowhere! It seemed to materialize out of thin air, a blur of tawny yellow, but in fact had been crouched on a tree limb, poised to strike. An ear-splitting screech trailed it downward.

A mountain lion, full-grown, savage,

one of nature's most efficient killing machines when roused. And it certainly was now, angered at the human who'd dared invade its territory.

The cat slammed into him with the force of a train and he hit the ground, stunned, the cougar landing atop him. The Winchester flew from his grip and landed a few feet away. He struggled with the beast, instinctively jamming a forearm into the cable-thick muscles of its neck to keep snapping fangs from finding his throat.

Claws raked his chest, shredding his shirt and leaving gaping scratches across his flesh. Its hot, raw-meat breath assailed his nostrils and saliva dripped on to his face. The beast was a good seven feet from nose to tail and sleekly muscled, incredibly powerful. At full strength he'd have little chance at besting it; in his present condition he had none.

Panic washed through his mind. Digging his fingers into the cougar's neck he squeezed but it had no effect.

The cat hissed and swiped at him with its great claws, almost raking flesh from his face. He managed to twist his head at the last minute and shove with all his strength, forcing the cat back a few inches, enough to keep his eyes from being gouged out.

Steve tried to roll, throw the beast off, but the cat weighed more than a full grown man and effectively pinned him to the ground. He gasped, strength quickly fading. It swiped at him again, claws sinking into his arm. The animal seemed more driven to kill him now, fevered by the scent of Steve's blood. He managed to poke it in an eye and the cat blinked, letting out a sharp hiss.

The move gave him a second's respite. He had one chance: draw his Peacemaker before the cougar mauled him to death. But to do that meant letting his guard down, giving the cat a chance to tear out his throat.

No choice. He would die anyway. He went for his gun.

The cat's fangs plunged towards this throat!

The Peacemaker jerked free, came half-up.

He was barely aware of pulling the trigger. A shot blasted and a welt ripped across the great cat's shoulder. Blood leaked across its tawny coat and the cat yowled in pain, surprise, fury. It leaped from him, scrambling away, vanishing into the countryside.

Steve collapsed, panting, pain radiating from every point of his body, Peacemaker falling to the ground. He'd gotten lucky for the second time in a day.

He rolled on to his side, sucking deep breaths and staring at the woods ahead. Scratches leaked blood.

Pushing himself up, he holstered the Peacemaker and located his Winchester. He started forward again, shirt in shreds, his will wavering, strength deserting him. He wouldn't make it. The attack had taken everything he had left. The distance was too great. He would die here, alone, Elana a thousand miles away.

Stop it! *You're Apache*! *Use that strength*!

Yes, Apache blood coursed through his veins. He was one of the 'people', strong, bred of tradition and sacred belief, part of the land itself, imbued with iron will and steely perseverance in the face of adversity. Nothing, *nothing*, neither man nor beast nor terrain could break his spirit. Steve told himself that over and over, struggling to silence the nagging voice of doubt deep within him.

He refused to give in, calling on the Grandfather above to give him strength, the crow to guide him, the spirits of the winds and whispering woods to protect him.

Another mile bled by. His heart felt thick in his chest, beating like muffled drums. Sweat stung his eyes. He began to shake.

The sky darkened, sun sinking behind the Rockies. A chill seeped into the air. Dusk swallowed the land, a soundless creeping thing. All around him silence, except for his fevered thoughts, the throbbing of his pulse, the beating of his staggered breath.

Two more miles slipped by. He would not reach town by nightfall, and though the last thing he wanted to do was stop he would be forced to make camp for the night.

Nights were cold and crystal clear in Wyoming. He would need to build a fire, though that came with risks: it might attract the cougar or some other predator, or it might draw the Indians if they returned, though that was less likely because they usually didn't attack at night.

It was a necessary risk or by morning he'd be in no shape to resume his journey.

After a brief rest, he gathered kindling he found by a deadfall and snapped brittle branches from cottonwoods, setting it in a pile. An armload of dried dead leaves provided a start for the fire. He dug a lucifer from his pocket and set the leaves and kindling aflame. Soon a fire roared, softening the darkness, warming him.

Somewhere in the darkness the crow cawed.

He sat next to the blaze, letting its warmth flow over him. Despite the heat he shivered uncontrollably.

He lay back, drawing up his knees and wrapping his arms about himself. His mind wandered, images of Elana, the Indians, the cougar rising up, hazy, retreating. He fell into a restless slumber —

He sat bolt upright. His heart pounded and at first he wasn't sure what had disturbed him. The night looked unusually black. The fire snapped and crackled and blazed with blood-red flame. The gurgling of the stream had become a peculiar gibbering laugh.

What was happening? An ominous feeling of dread shivered through his being. He felt something drawing close, something out there in the darkness, in the night, all around him. A presence, like Indian spirits, dark spirits.

He grew aware of something else. He felt no pain. He looked down to find his wound had vanished! He touched the spot where it had been, fingers trembling slightly. The scratches were gone as well.

Confusion gripped him and he stood, hand drifting to his Peacemaker — it was no longer at his hip! An empty holster hung there. Vague panic edged into his mind.

A movement to the side caught his attention.

The crow! Twice its normal size, it flew out of the darkness, screeching, wings beating. He gasped and the monstrous bird came straight for him, only to dissolve into a thousand sparkles of black light that rained to the ground and dissolved.

'What's happening?' Steve yelled, panic growing.

Muffled beating arose like the thunder of Indian drums, throbbing low, rising until the sound became deafening.

Beating, beating, beating, filling him with terror. It pounded against his ears, his soul, coming from all around him, from within.

He pressed his hands to his ears, trying to force the din away. It was no use. It only grew louder, threatening to crush his skull.

Wings. Not drums. The beating of huge invisible wings.

Beating, pounding, thundering. Through space and memory. Wings of doom, wings of death.

On the ground before him, where the great bird had dissolved, blackness sizzled across the dead leaves and pine needles. It geysered, swirling, sparkles of black spinning, spinning, spinning, falling together, coalescing into a figure of blackness.

A chill shuddered down his back at the sight of the spectral figure. The apparition, garbed in a black robe and cowl, features hidden, stood before him unmoving, robe fluttering in the breeze. A black mist crept over the ground, pooling at its hidden feet.

The sight dredged a deep terror from his soul. No Indian figure this; the ghostly bird was Apache but this apparition was an image born of the white blood flowing through his veins, a grim spectre who collected a body when it knocked at death's door. He remembered the image from some book his father had shown him, the death angel.

The figure's arm drifted up, a white hand slipping from beneath the folds of cloth, pointing at him.

'Nooo!' he yelled, taking a step backward.

The beating of wings ceased. The air went deathly still. All Steve heard was the muffled throbbing of his own heart.

The figure glided forward, black mist slithering about it like black snakes.

'What do you want from me?' he shouted and the figure stopped. A gentle laugh ululated from unseen lips.

A woman's laugh.

'Why are you here?' he demanded.

'Tell me! Am I dead?'

In response, delicate white hands went to the cowl, pulling it away from its face.

Steve's heart hammered as shock filled him. He stared at the figure's face, a beautiful face with fine features, slightly upturned nose and full mouth, crystal blue eyes, the cloud of blonde hair that cascaded to her shoulders.

Elana!

'Elena,' he whispered. A strange sense of peace wandered through him as he spoke her name and he suddenly wondered why he had ever been afraid of the figure. There was no need to be. It was Elana, his Elana. But how had she found him? Why was she here? Confusion rose in his mind and he slowly shook his head. 'Elena, what are you doing here?'

The girl moved a step forward and he suddenly noticed a strange dullness in her blue eyes, an emptiness he didn't remember. 'Elena . . . ' He reached for her but she shook her head.

'No, Steve. Do not touch me.'

'Elena, I don't understand.' The dread returned, a simmering vague fear. What was wrong with her? Why didn't she want him to touch her?

'I have come to say goodbye . . . '

'What? What do you mean 'goodbye'?'

'Watch the crow, my love. Let him be your guide. Remember I love you and go on.' Her words came soft and low, dissolving into the breeze.

'No, don't leave me. Elana, don't — '

'Goodbye . . . ' she whispered, stepping back. He leaped forward, reaching for her —

But touched nothing. Her form melted into the shape of the great black crow and fluttered off, leaving emptiness and slithering black mist.

'Elanaaaa!' he screamed, voice dragging out, laden with crushing sorrow and want. 'Don't leave me, don't leave — '

Steve awoke with a start, sitting bolt upright. He gasped, heart hammering, emotion clogging his throat, sweat trickling down his face. Beside him the fire crackled and sputtered, flames of yellow and orange. The musky scent of burning wood filled his nostrils. At his shoulder, the wound ached powerfully. Scratches criss-crossed his chest and arm. A chill swept through him.

The fever. That's all it had been. Delirium wrapped in the folds of a dream, a nightmare. 'Elena,' he mouthed, putting his face in his hands. For long moments he shook with fever and cold. His head reeled, hazy images of the great black bird and spectral figure of Elana flittering before his mind.

Head lifting, he searched the darkness for some sign of the crow, saw nothing. He didn't expect to. Dread simmered within him, fueled by a vague sense of doom, of hidden meaning to the nightmare.

Minutes passed, suspended, silent. He lay back down, but sleep came in snatched moments and restless fragments for the remainder of the night.

4

MORNING dawned after an eternity.

False dawn greys daubed the sky and Steve Matthews came from a restless slumber. Sitting up, he placed his face in his hands, nauseated and weak. His clothes were soaked with sweat and he felt alternately chilled and heated. The flesh around the wound looked red and angry and flies buzzed around it.

For long moments he didn't move, struggling to gather enough strength to gain his feet. It would be easy to lie back down, let death steal over him, end the suffering.

You are Apache!

Yes, he was. He had to go on, fight to his last breath. He was no quitter and Elana was waiting for him.

Elana.

As her name touched his lips and the strange dread simmered in his belly, he struggled to pinpoint a reason for it, but it lay just out of conscious reach, something mystical, almost, frightening and confusing.

The sun blinked over the horizon and the woodland glowed with brilliant hues of orange and gold. Autumn leaves blazed bright with color, sparkled with dew, frost melting. With a deep breath, he heaved himself to his feet. His legs felt rubbery at first, but steadied some as he moved about. He hefted his Winchester, eyeing the trail south. He reckoned he had roughly four or five miles to go before reaching the outskirts of Deadeye.

The crow returned. It cawed as if with encouragement as it glided above him and he felt strangely glad of its presence.

He started along the trail, steps slow, each taken with infinite care. A stumble now might spell doom; he didn't know if he had the strength to get up. After a few hundred yards the Winchester slipped from his grasp, suddenly too heavy to carry.

The trail jittered. Trees swayed like drunken saloon girls. Sweat flowed more freely with each step.

A mile trickled away. Another.

Increasingly he wondered what drove him, what force of will carried him on against all odds. Elana. Yes, Elana. He could not let her down, leave her alone.

Elana.

Dread washed through him again. Why was it attached to her name?

The sun climbed higher, warming the land, and he paused, pressing his eyes shut, letting it flow over him, gathering his strength. He barely felt his legs beneath him. His breath staggered out in ragged, thready gasps.

Only another mile or two, he told himself. Only another mile or two.

Forward. His progress slowed to a crawl.

The crow circled and screeched,

snapping him from his spell every time unconsciousness threatened to wash over him, every time his focus wandered.

You're Apache!

Yes, Apache. One of 'the people'.

The trail thinned of trees and the rise to his right softened. Soon it melted away and the land evened out. Close, now. Close to town, to help.

There!

On the horizon he spotted a house, windows shining in the sunlight. A vision? A mirage? A taunting of his fevered brain? Perhaps. Perhaps it wasn't there at all.

He stumbled towards it, hope renewed, fueling what little strength he had remaining. It had to be real. It had to be.

Drawing closer to the house, he saw it was no mirage. It was real, the gates of Heaven to a damned soul.

With renewed effort he trudged towards it. He had made it, he had —

He stumbled, going down, still a few hundred yards from the house. The burst of strength proved fleeting, a flare of brightness before darkness overcame all. He had nothing left. The fall seemed infinite and torturous. He slammed into the dirt, pain wracking his wound, exhausted.

He fought to push himself up, unsuccessful. He would die, now, so close to his goal, so close to freedom. The crow screeched overhead and through fevered vision he looked up, seeing its black shape glide across the sun like the shadow of death. Brightness stung his eyes and he pressed them shut. He listened, listened to the muffled beating of his heart, to the murmuring of blood coursing through his veins. So this was what death felt like. It wasn't painful, merely sapping, a trickling away of the senses, a peculiar heightening of awareness. A door creeping open, inviting him in . . . inviting him . . .

A sound. Somewhere. Why was

it invading his death? Why was it disturbing him?

Again it came, off to his left. A crunching of leaves, a footfall. Indians? Mountain cat? Did it matter?

No, one set of steps, furtive, cautious, picked with infinite care. Whoever it was had spotted him lying on the ground and was approaching gingerly.

His eyes fluttered open, vision blurred. A dim shape floated before him, a smallish figure, holding something in each hand.

A basket of some sort, he determined, in the left, a rifle in the other.

A woman. Walking slowly towards him.

She wore some sort of odd dress, something foreign that glittered with gold and green designs in the sun.

'Help . . . me . . . ' he mouthed, words barely audible. He reached out and she stopped. 'Help me, please . . . '

He collapsed, face hitting the ground, senses deserting him. Blackness invaded his mind and the last thing he remembered was the woman bending over him.

★ ★ ★

She shouldn't have brought him here. She shouldn't have helped him at all.

She remembered what happened the last time a man came to her home, how he murdered Jason and left her heart bloated with a great swelling sorrow and endless pain, bottomless loneliness.

Sarah Cheng set the basket of herbs, which she had gone back out to collect because the man had been too heavy for her to drag without using both arms, on a table. It was all she could do to drag him from the field to the small office. She had collected her rifle as well, placing it in ready should the man awaken and try to hurt her.

She shouldn't have brought him here.

The thought plagued her mind. She shouldn't have cared. But that would be what Jason would want her to do and she had an obligation to his spirit, his kindness. He deserved that honor and she would bite back her fear.

Standing near the desk, she gazed about the office, a room she had rarely entered since Jason died. The pain still lived inside this room. The ghosts still lingered. While grief had lost some of its intensily over the months, she still hated the emptiness this room held, the awful memories. She missed his warm voice, his soothing manner. She missed his laughter, his gentleness. She had gained so much only to lose it again. It was not fair and if she saw the one-eyed man again she vowed she would kill him for that, for Jason. It was the only way to free his spirit — and hers.

She had been alone for so long now. Memories were merely ghosts of the night, insubstantial fleeting things that haunted her in weak moments. At times grief returned in waves and crushed her, sent hot tears streaking down her face.

Jason's compassion for the suffering of his fellow man had killed him. It might kill her as well, if this man turned out to be like the other.

Sarah's gaze swept to the man lying on the steel examination table. She could delay no longer, for the man had sunk deep into fever; he muttered strange things, something about a woman he loved and some great black bird of death. She did not understand such things, but supposed it was delirium causing him to speak in that way.

Going to him, she peered at his face. He was darker than most white men she encountered, indicating some sort of mix. Indian, she judged, though she was not sure which tribe. He appeared to be roughly her age, about thirty, and his face was kind, though haggard, flushed. He did not have the look of a murderer, the way the other had. If he had she would have let him die where he had fallen and buried him later, despite her promise to Jason's spirit.

Sliding a tray of surgical instruments next to the table, she selected a pair of sharp scissors and began to snip away the man's shirt around the wound. The fabric was caked with browned blood. This man suffered from two things, claw wounds caused by some sort of animal — most likely a mountain lion, she decided — and a more serious puncture created by an arrow. She saw the broken-off shaft protruding from the angry purple hole. Fly larvae dotted the livid flesh. If it weren't cleaned, the wound would soon be infested with soft white maggots.

She finished clipping away the shirt and discarded the shreds of material. He moaned softly and she studied him for a moment, wondering whether he would wake up. No, she decided, he was merely feverish, stirring restlessly.

She daubed the wound with carbolic, cleaning it thoroughly of the larvae and dried blood. Fresh red blood bubbled around the broken arrow shaft and she wiped it away. Good. That would purge the wound. Mixing a gentle antiseptic of permanganate of potash by dissolving purple crystals into a dipper of water, she applied it to the area. She knew a great deal about doctoring, both the white and Chinese ways. Jason had taught her much and what he had not she absorbed from *Lancet* and other journals. Although Lister's theory of sepsis and antisepsis had been published in 1867, few doctors other than Jason employed such methods, even as much as sixteen years later. But she did and believed in the unseen bacteria that infested open wounds and brought on the ravages of infection and blood poisoning, the corrupting horror of gangrene.

She paused and felt his pulse. Rapid, weak: the fever had taken hold in a vicious way. She wondered if he had made it to her only to die on the table. She uttered a Chinese prayer and lifted the scalpel from the tray, holding it with a steady hand above his wound.

Removing the arrowhead and broken shaft might prove difficult. She knew something of arrows from the times she had assisted Jason. Removed improperly, the flint head could do more damage than a bullet.

With great care, she slid the scalpel into the angry hot flesh. The man stirred, groaned, and she withdrew a fraction, then began to probe again. She had never actually attempted surgery before, merely observed Jason doing it, so there was a high risk she would cause this man more harm than good. But without the attempt, he would die anyway, so she saw little choice.

Sweat dripped from her forehead and blood soaked her hands. The small muscles in the back of her neck and shoulders ached from tension. It took nearly half an hour to remove the arrowhead and length of shaft. The man stirred and moaned constantly, the sharp pain penetrating his stupor and she worried he would suddenly snap awake and her hand would slip, causing serious damage. But he did not and she felt a surge of relief when the arrowhead finally lifted out.

She set about cleaning the area with permanganate and sealing his wound with a plaster. Lastly, she treated the scratches then bundled his left arm in a sling.

After scrubbing her hands clean of blood and washing off the scissors and scalpel, she placed a knitted afghan with Chinese designs over him, leaving him resting on the table for the time being.

Going to her basket, she selected a number of herbs, from which she would brew a Chinese medicinal tea that she would force down the man's throat as soon as he was able to take it. The immediate danger had passed, but fever and infection might claim him all the same.

Herbs she needed in hand, Sarah went to the kitchen and located the teapot, which she filled with water from the sink pump and set on the cast-iron stove. She placed the herbs in the pot to brew and soon fragrant steam wafted up.

Perhaps the man would live. Perhaps he would not. She had done all she could and that was the best to be hoped for. She had fulfilled her promise to Jason's memory. If the man turned out to be a criminal she prayed this time he would simply kill her and not leave her to the horrible loneliness, the empty nights and silent rooms.

She uttered an uneasy laugh, her dark eyes pained. Looking out the window she saw deepening shadows creep across the land. Dusk. The lonely time. The time for ghosts to awaken, haunt her. Seven months had dragged by since he left her, but she swore she saw him in evening shadows sometimes, saw him standing in the dying light of the day, smiling at her, entreating her to go on, to forget the grief and emptiness. He had always been more concerned about her than himself, the kindest, gentlest man she had ever met, at a time she thought all men lived only to use her as a slave, to whip and to lie with. She missed him with all her being. How could she ever be happy again? Half the town hated her for being Chinese while others called her a whore for not being Jason's legal wife. But this house was all she had; she had nowhere else to go, no place to hide. She would die rather than return to San Francisco and slavery.

Happiness seemed a distant unreachable dream. All she had now was mere existence, doing chores for the few in town who treated her with kindness, a small amount of cash Jason had left her. Nothing else.

Except hate. Hate for the man who murdered Jason, hate for the man who had taken so much from her when she had so little. An impotent hate because she had no way of finding the man, killing him.

The teapot blew a shrill whistle, tearing her from her thoughts. She went to the stove and removed it from the burner. The man would not be able to drink it for hours, if ever, but it was prepared and that was enough.

A sound from the other room made her start. She was not used to sounds at dusk and it chilled her. A moan. Her hand went to her heart, feeling its sped-up beating.

Another sound. What was it? Was it possible the stranger had awakened so soon? She doubted it but decided she had better check.

She headed for the office as shadows pooled in the house, shadows that uttered silent warnings and made her pause just beyond the kitchen doorway. Another sound from the room and she started forward again, ignoring the ramblings of shadows and praying the night would pass quickly, the way she did each evening. It never did.

* * *

The great black bird arose from the swirling black mist. It fluttered through his nightmare, an evil spirit that foretold death. Where was he? Lying on the ground? That's the last thing he remembered. But something looked different. He saw no fire, no light, merely darkness, a landscape crowded with charred trees upon which sprouted the faces of the hardcases he had killed, their eyes hollow, damning, mouths gaping with silent screams.

Panic swelled in his mind. He looked down to see the wounds at his shoulder bleeding liberally, streamers of blood streaking down his chest and side.

The bird swooped up, wings beating with the sound of thunder. It landed before him, vanishing in a great billowing black cloud. The cloud drifted away, and Elana, dressed in the black robe, stood before him. Her face looked hollow, eyes pale and distant.

Her voice drifted out, a whisper. 'Beware the Widow Maker . . . '

'Elana!' he yelled, reaching for her, but she seemed too far away to touch, though she stood right before him.

A harsh laugh echoed through the black mist and her face dissolved, melting into the features of another — a man, large and powerful, his one eye roving. 'Your end is near, boy,' the figure rasped. 'I'm coming for you . . . '

Steve stepped back, hand sweeping for his gun, bringing it up as if in slow motion. Leveling, he jerked the trigger. Bullets punched holes in the outlaw's chest, but he merely laughed. The slugs had no effect.

'Your time has come . . . ' The man took a step towards him and Steve shrieked, a wail that shocked him from his nightmare.

He sat bolt upright, gasping, sweat streaking down his face. White-hot pain stabbed his shoulder, piercing deep to the bone. He groaned, clutching at it, feeling a bandage of some sort. He slowly opened his eyes, vision blurry. The room appeared foreign, unreal, jittering. He threw the blanket off his legs and swung them off the table, barely having enough strength to do so.

Where was he? The last thing he recollected was reaching a house, collapsing just short of it. Someone . . . an image struggled to form in his mind. A woman, a woman with a rifle and a basket. Had she brought him here?

Sudden thunder crashed in his head and he pressed his hands to his ears, trying to block it out. The beating of the great black wings! Before him the bird appeared, screeching, flying towards him. This was no dream! He was awake! No, delirium, he told himself, shaking with fever. He slid off the table, stumbling towards the bird, which dissolved as he reached out.

The thunderous beating of wings grew louder, louder louder.

Movement — at the door!

His gaze rose. A figure stood there, watching him.

He struggled to focus, but couldn't.

'Who are you?' he shouted, stepping

forward, panic seizing his mind. '*Who are you*?'

The figure came forward a step and he saw the face clearly. It was him! The one-eyed outlaw from his nightmare! That's what Elana had been trying to warn him about. The Widow Maker was here, was going to kill him!

Steve's eyes narrowed. He summoned all his strength, hand sweeping for the Peacemaker at his hip. He felt its comforting grip, snapped it from its holster in an anaemic draw that caused the weapon to waver on its way up.

The beating crescendoed. Hammering. Crushing. The one-eyed man laughed, drawing his own gun.

Steve leveled the Peacemaker.

★ ★ ★

Sarah heard more noises coming from the office as she made her way down the hall. Though it seemed impossible the man had awoken, it was obvious he had. He must have possessed an incredible will, much hidden strength to have recovered enough to awaken so quickly.

A scream. She paused, startled. Why had he called out in such a manner? There was utter terror in that scream. Was the man conscious or merely delirious, ranting?

She went forward, stopping again just beyond the door to the office. A chill went through her. A premonition of some sort, a warning. But why? She hesitated, then assured herself he could not harm her; he was far too weak.

Taking small steps, she reached the doorway and peered in. He stood in the center of the room, appearing frightened and unsteady. He muttered something, but she could not hear what it was. His gaze swung to her, eyes wild with fear.

She uttered a sharp gasp, frozen as he went for his gun.

The gun came up, leveling on her face. Her eyes went wide and her heart seemed to stop as she stared down its threatening bore.

He was going to kill her!

5

SEVEN months had passed since Brace Carrigan last set eyes on Deadeye; even then he'd only passed through. He recollected that day as if it had been yesterday, the day that guard from the Stalwright stage put a bullet into his hide and he'd gotten that doc to dig it out. The wound had healed up fine and dandy. The doc had done a good piece of work. Too bad he had to kill him. Too bad, indeed.

Brace uttered an emotionless laugh at the memory. He had done that Chinagirl a favor, he reckoned. The man would have only done her wrong.

I'll kill you, you stupid barwhore!

A memory invaded his mind; words shuddered from the past and, as he sat overlooking the town, he stiffened in the saddle. It drew him back, through dark mists and black pain. Hazy images, clearing, brittle. Memories of a boy, a cowering, bitter, frightened boy of twelve, possibly thirteen; it was hard to recollect, now, because he rarely let himself indulge in such reveries.

A door burst open, banging against the wall, shuddering with the sound of a gunshot. His pa filled the doorway, wildness in his eyes, then staggered inside, drunk as all get out. The smell of cheap perfume clung to him like sin, mixed with sweat and manure.

'Where you been?' his mother asked. A sweet voice, gentle but strained, a woman pushed to her limits by a man who drank too much and spent his wages on bardoves rather than food for his family. Pa had met Ma in a saloon, that's what he had told Brace. But Brace didn't care because she was there when he needed her. Pa never was. So it really wasn't her fault Brace took to the urges he did, the surges of meanness that sizzled through him like a hot branding iron, the overwhelming desire to hurt things, make them take his own pain, his own emptiness.

'None 'a your goddamn business!' His pa's shout jangled him, but the snapping *crack*! of his backhand across his mother's face made his blood run cold. That blow struck her as though it had struck him, and he felt her pain as he cowered behind a big trunk in the parlor, watching. His mother staggered under the blow and blood trickled over her lips. Brace felt the burning surge of rage take him and he felt oddly powerless at the same time. The sight of blood twisted something in his soul, made his nostrils twitch and his heart thunder.

Blood. It wasn't the first time he noticed how red and shiny it looked, how mesmerizing. Blood. A pulling inside him, stronger, stronger, flowing over him like a chilled ocean. Cold. So cold. And dark, with shifting treacherous undertows, black tides. A sense of destiny pervaded the day, though he had no idea why he felt that way. But something was about to change and he knew from that moment on his life would be forced in an unchangeable direction.

Blood. He wanted to see more, touch it, taste it. But not his mother's. Oh, no, he loved her with unwavering devotion. When Pa beat her, Brace felt helpless, torn. The few times he'd interfered Pa had pounded him silly.

Pa was a big man, bigger than anyone in town; the few who had raised a hand against him in bar fights, or tried to protect Ma when he hit her in public, had met with instant death. Always self-defence, folks trying to interfere with his God-given husbandly right. Even the marshal feared his drunken rages.

The sense of destiny struck him again. This fight looked worse than most and he reckoned Pa was drunker than usual. He saw smears of bright red lipstick staining the collar of his boiled shirt. His mother saw them, too, and he saw tears hidden behind her eyes, rage, finality.

'You'll never do this to me again!' she shouted, face pinched, tears streaking over her cheeks. A madness came over her then; Brace saw it, knew it, because he felt it himself. She lunged for a knife on the table and Brace's heart thundered. A fevered excitement rose within him the way it did when he killed coyotes that ventured near the house. He delighted in killing, watching things suffer. He suspected his Pa had seen that in him, and it had made him hate Brace all the more. He had overheard his Pa tell Mr Baker at the general store: 'The boy's got bad blood, Sam, I can tell it. He likes to kill things, likes to hurt them. Think he's got a goddamned devil inside him!'

Pa was right; and Brace wanted to hurt him most of all.

His mother grabbed the knife, swung it around. Steel streaked through the air in a silver blur.

Brace's father, drunk but still capable, caught her wrist in mid-air and forced it around. Brace's elation turned to horror.

The knife plunged deep into his mother's chest! She screamed, the sound quickly turning into a gurgle. He saw more blood, then, fountains of it, on his mother's dress, his Pa's hands. Glittering, shiny scarlet blood. But his heart sank at the sight because he knew his mother, the one person he cared about, was dead.

Rage overtaking him, he leaped from behind the trunk, screaming at his pa, tears rushing from his eyes. 'I'll kill you, you bastard! I'll kill you!'

His father whirled, shock widening his eyes, the color drained from his face. 'She tried to kill me, boy! You saw it! I didn't mean — '

Those were the last of his words Brace heard. He snatched a scattergun from the wall rack, the one he had loaded yesterday just on the chance he'd get to shoot a coyote, and swung it around. It was bulky, cumbersome, and when he triggered a shot it bucked him backward. He stumbled, going down on his rear. His gaze rose to his pa, who just stood there, a gaping hole in his chest spouting blood. Brace watched the blood flow with grisly fascination. A strange coldness moved through his soul, as if the feeling of destiny had suddenly been appeased. Pa crumbled to the floor, gasping, then going deathly still.

For a frozen moment, Brace stared. Then he laughed uncontrollably until the dusk came and he fell asleep on the floor, all emotion leeched from his being.

'Brace?' A voice penetrated his reverie. He blinked, seeing Shale peering at him with a curious look.

'You off again?' she asked, giving him that damned toothless smile of hers.

He took a deep breath and his one eye focused on the town. 'Reckon I was.'

'We gonna have some fun or what?' snapped Bertha, nudging her head towards the town. 'Got me a notion to be right kind to some lucky fella.' She uttered a husky laugh and her chins jiggled.

Brace tensed a notch, disturbed by his memories. He looked at the mannish gang member. Bertha even made him edgy sometimes. Her menfolk usually weren't no good to anybody after she got done with them. He had to admire her for that. He nodded, looking at the town. 'Reckon that's what we came for.'

'Let's git a move on then!' Bertha bellowed a 'Yah!' and heeled her horse into motion. The rest followed suit, Brace lingering behind with Shale, who gave him another look.

'What is it, Brace?' Her brow crinkled.

'Nothin'. Just recollectin' the last time we passed through this area, after robbin' that stage.' His fingers drifted to a spot at his shoulder.

'Reckon nobody'll be gettin' shot this time, Brace.'

An evil smile oiled his lips. 'Wouldn't go that far — Yah!' He sent his horse into a gallop, arrowing for the town.

Deadeye was a lattice-work affair of buildings sporting false fronts and stout construction. Boards were thick and dwellings were built to withstand icy winters and summer storms. Deep ruts lined the wide main street and dust swirled beneath horses' hooves. Clods of manure littered the thoroughfare. A livery, general store, scattered shops and marshal's office stood near the town's entrance. Residences and a hotel took up the remainder of Deadeye.

Dusk sent elongated shadows stretching across the street, pooling in alleys. An eerie stillness gripped the town. For the briefest of moments Brace Carrigan felt something he'd rarely felt before: premonition. An impending sense of destiny that told him something would happen soon, something that might change the course of his life forever. He'd felt the same thing the day he'd killed his Pa and he felt it now.

105

He shook it off, wondering what the goddamn hell had come over him. Wasn't like him, but he reckoned he hadn't been quite the same since that bullet punched a hole in him seven months ago. As if whatever that destiny was it had been set in motion the day he killed that doc. Now it felt stronger, closer. Stalking him. He didn't like it, but it was nothing he could put a bullet in. Yet. He spat, shaking his head.

Shale peered at him again. 'Brace, you ain't actin' like yourself.'

As he looked at her, his eye roved. 'Don't know what it is, Shale, but I got me a feelin'.'

'What kinda feelin'?' The toothless woman looked puzzled.

He shrugged.

A crow landed atop a building ledge just across from him. His attention went to it and the ominous sense of premonition strengthened. With sudden fury he drew his gun and fired at the bird, which screeched and flew off.

Shale cocked an eyebrow but said nothing.

The others shot glances at their leader and he waved a hand. 'Hitch up here. Saloon's just yonder.'

Dismounting, they tethered their mounts to the rail.

'Hey, Brace, marshal's office's just a building down.' Calamity Annie nodded towards the horses. 'Maybe we should put 'em in an alley or somethin'.'

Brace smiled. 'Got a notion it ain't gonna matter.'

Dusk deepened and the street grew nearly deserted. Hanging lanterns glowed to life and windows brightened with buttery light. Deadeye would sleep for the night, except for the saloon, from which could be heard the sounds of a honky-tonk and bawdy laughter.

It had been a while since Brace let his gals put on the elephant, so he reckoned they deserved it.

They stepped on to the boardwalk, boots clomping on dusty boards, and headed for the saloon.

A man and woman, arm in arm, chanced to stroll on to the boardwalk a few blocks down.

Brace's gaze locked on them and his lips drew into a line. Shale noticed the look and let out a chuckle.

Brace took the lead, hand drifting over the butt of his Schofield. He halted in front of the couple and tipped his hat to the woman. 'Ma'am.' He gave her a smile that held little warmth.

The man, a weaselly little fellow in Brace's estimation, ran his gaze up and down the outlaw. 'Sir, what is your business with us?' he demanded in a proud cock voice that sent a silver of irritation into Brace's nerves.

Brace eyed the woman, whose face had taken on a look of vague fear. 'He'll just disappoint you, ma'am. I can't let that happen.' Words barely out of his mouth, his Schofield cleared leather. His finger twitched on the trigger. A shot rang through the street and the suited man's face took on a startled expression. His eyes rolled up and he crumpled to the boardwalk, a hole between his eyes.

The woman shrieked, an agonized wail of horror and sorrow. She didn't stop until Bertha stepped up and crossed her jaw with a blocky fist. The woman dropped beside her dead husband. Bertha drew her gun, aiming at the unconscious figure.

Brace gave her a brisk wave of his hand. 'You know better'n that.' He stared at the fallen woman, pity in his eye. She was saved and that was good. He would save them all.

Bertha rolled her eyes, but holstered her Smith & Wesson.

'Best get them off the boardwalk 'fore someone comes,' said Calamity Annie, who bent and shoved her hands under the woman's arms. She dragged her into the alley while the triplets hoisted up the dead man and dumped him beside his wife.

'Someone mighta heard that shot

and the one before, Brace,' said Shale. 'Maybe we best find us another town.'

Brace shook his head. 'When the marshal finds 'em the party'll just be gettin' started.' He walked towards the saloon and the girls hesitated only a beat before following, used to his dark moods and rarely questioning his decisions.

A haze of Durham smoke hung in the saloon. A man with an armband banged away at a honky-tonk and bargirls flittered about, hanging on to the arms of gamblers, tinhorns and locals who found their luck on the upswing. Sawdust covered the floor, lumpy in spots, and ground beneath Brace's boots. He saw poker, chuck-a-luck and faro games in progress, but he had never been much for gambling. He preferred a bellyful of whiskey and the occasional whore.

He went to the bar and the girls sat on stools to either side of him. The barkeep, a burly man in his late forties, eyed them with a suspicious glint, and some other notion Brace couldn't quite figure until the man spoke.

'We don't serve ladies.' He nodded at the girls.

A sudden flash of movement and Calamity Annie had her Smith & Wesson jammed against the 'keep's forehead. She smiled a mousy smile. 'There's been a change in company policy.' The words came cold and delivered with six-gun insurance.

The 'keep looked startled and sweat beaded on his brow. 'Reckon I can live with that . . . ' He said it in a shaky voice.

Calamity Annie lowered the gun and shoved it into her holster, then sat back on her stool. Pulling out the dime novel stashed in her belt, she opened it and began scanning the pages.

Bertha let out a guffaw and slapped Annie on the shoulder. 'Hell, sister, you shore got a way with the gents!'

The barkeep set out seven glasses but filled only six. Brace pushed his glass away and grabbed the bottle. 'Reckon

I'll be runnin' a tab.' Something in his eye told the barkeep it wasn't a request.

Bertha downed her whiskey in one gulp. 'Hell, I'ma ready for a ruckus!' She stalked off and Brace saw her snatch some unlucky fellow from his seat and haul him towards the stairs. The tinhorn didn't want to go, but Bertha, though she looked like five miles of bad trail, could be right persuasive.

Annie kept at her book, sipping whiskey occasionally.

One of the triplets, April — or was it May? hell, sometimes he couldn't tell the damn difference — became annoyed with the banging of piano keys and let sail with her bolas. The weapon knocked the key-tickler in the back of the head and he flipped off his stool as if he been poleaxed.

She walked over to him, gave him a kick and retrieved her weapon, hitching it to her belt. The three sisters then went to a table and began playing poker.

Shale, sitting beside Brace, took swigs of her whiskey, letting the amber liquid ride over her gums before swallowing. She sat in contemplative silence a short time then peered at Brace, who stared into his whiskey bottle.

'What's eatin' you, Brace? I ain't seen you act this far off for quite a spell. An' don't give me no bullspit about gettin' shot at, neither.'

He shrugged, a slight sneer on his lips. 'Can't rightly say. Reckon I got me the fever on. Got the urge to kill someone.'

'You just did; that ain't it.'

He gave her a glance, then took a gulp from the bottle. 'You tell me, then.'

'Reckon I don't know. But there's somethin', has been ever since that day at the doc's. That Chinagal didn't put no curse on you, did she?'

'Maybe she did at that — hell!' He slapped the counter and the barkeep jolted, looking worried. Brace reminded himself to shoot the man on the way out. 'This is s'posed to be a goddamned party!' He swung off the stool and grabbed a dove who happened to be passing by. 'Right, purdy lady?' She gave him a fearful expression and he grinned, taking another gulp of whiskey and letting it dribble into his scraggy beard.

'You best have lots of greenbacks,' the girl said without much conviction. Her cheeks were daubed with coral, eyes shaded with kohl — a look he rightly liked. He always was one for life on the exaggerated side.

'Reckon you'll take what you get.' He stood, taking her towards the stairs.

A shout stopped him in his tracks. He stood motionless, the dove at his side.

'You best let her go, fella,' said the marshal, who stood just inside the door, hand poised above his Peacemaker. 'I mean it.'

'Do you, now?' Brace slowly turned. Shale swung around on her seat and

Calamity Annie looked up from her dime novel.

Brace's eye settled on the lawman and two deputies standing behind him. The marshal flinched just a hair and Brace liked that. 'Why, Marshal, we're just havin' us a good time.'

Disgust turned the marshal's face. 'By killing that man out in the alley? His wife came runnin' in screaming all hell 'bout what you and your . . . friends done. You just let the girl go and come peaceably.'

Brace gave a short chuckle and pushed the dove away.

Two more deputies burst in the back. Brace saw them from the corner of his eye.

Calamity Annie closed her book and tucked it into her belt. Shale set her whiskey glass on the counter and stood. The triplets laid their cards on the table.

Brace laughed. The marshal seemed somewhat taken aback by the out-of-place expression; his eyes narrowed.

That's when Brace drew.

The outlaw's hand slapped for the Schofield; it appeared in his grip as if by some magical force. He triggered a hasty shot that punched into the marshal's thigh.

The lawman blurted a yell and the deputies went for their guns.

Patrons, frightened, yelling, dived beneath tables. It would be the last thing the lawman wanted, Brace figured, a shoot-out with innocent folk involved. Which was exactly why he had given it to him. It afforded Brace the advantage. The deputies and marshal had to be cautious lest they accidentally kill someone innocent; Brace didn't give a damn who he hit, long as it weren't women.

The marshal had made a serious miscalculation in judgement in coming in here after Brace and his gang and now he would pay for it.

The lawmen's guns came out, searching for targets.

Brace dove for cover behind the

piano, as a bullet ripped into the floorboards where he'd stood not a second before. The slug kicked up a cloud of saw-dust.

The triplets jumped to their feet, throwing over the table, ducking behind it. Bullets ricocheted, splintering wood, embedding themselves in walls. Glasses shattered with crashing jangles.

Shale leaped over the bar, shoving a startled bar-keep aside. The barkeep lunged for a scattergun beneath the counter and she put a bullet between his eyes. He hit the floor with a heavy thud, lay still.

Brace delivered staccato shots and the marshal, limping his way for cover, jolted in his step. A bullet shattered the lawdog's shoulder blade and Brace followed with another shot that completely separated his spine. He went down in a cloud of sawdust, blood splattering the boards.

Drawn by the shots, Bertha appeared at the top of the stairs, jerking up her trousers and buckling on her gunbelt

She scurried down at a deceptive speed for a large woman, pumping shots at the deputies, who had taken cover behind tables or crates piled in the back. One lawman ducked behind a small stage that sometimes featured bargirl dancers.

A dove shrieked and one of the triplets straightened, whirling her bolas above her head. She let the weapon fly; it wrapped itself about the dove's throat, who stopped screaming abruptly, prying at the cords in panic.

A deputy took aim on the triplet and blasted a shot. A crimson blotch splattered across the triplet's side and she froze, toppled over the table. Spasming, she gasped raspy breaths.

'Goddammit, Brace!' yelled Shale, worry weighting her voice. 'They shot June!' Shale drew a bead on the deputy, firing before the man could quite get back to cover. He jerked, the slug gouging a furrow across his neck. With a yip, he slapped a hand over the wound and ducked down.

Doves ran and panicked patrons tried foolish dashes for the door. They only got in the way of bullets, though the doves were luckier because Brace wouldn't shoot them. Two gamblers fell dead under a hail of lead from Bertha's Smith & Wesson before they made it five feet.

A deputy retaliated with a shot, missing. Slugs whined throughout the barroom, neither side particularly careful whom they hit now in the fever of the fracas. Bullets shattered mirrors and punched holes in tables, paintings, walls, the bar, and piano. Splinters flew and glass shards lacerated the air.

Brace suddenly didn't care for the way things were going. One of his gang was down, and the deputies were proving more skilled than he'd counted on. He shouted an order for the girls to get out and the lawman with the neck wound jumped from cover, endeavoring to stop them as they scurried towards the batwings. A bullet from Calamity Annie's gun ended his life.

The remaining triplets tried to drag their sister, but Brace shouted, 'She's done for, goddammit! Leave 'er!' They gave it little thought; June was gouting blood from her mouth and nothing on earth could save her. If they stayed bullets would put them in the same condition.

Shale and Calamity Annie, blasting lead, made it through the batwings. April, May and Bertha sent a volley of bullets at the hunkered deputies, who returned fire. Brace dove outside, followed by the rest of his gang.

The saloon was a shambles, bodies, splinters and broken glass lay everywhere. The three remaining deputies bolted from cover on the heels of the bandits. They plunged through the batwings and dashed for the shelter of rain barrels and water-troughs.

Night had flooded the street with shadows and patches of butter-colored light from hanging lanterns, giving scant illumination, making aim difficult. A deputy jumped up and fired at Bertha, who lagged slightly behind. He missed but April did not. She flung a bolas at him and the balls cracked him in the face. He dropped his Peacemaker and clutched at his crushed gushing nose. A hail of bullets followed, cutting the man down before he had time to take a step.

The other deputies bolted from point to point, triggering shots and endeavoring to get closer to the bandits, stop them from reaching their horses.

Brace and his women sent a hail of lead backwards, keeping the lawmen off balance. One deputy went down, rolling into the street, a bullet in his gut.

The gang reached their mounts and leaped into the saddle, reining around.

A bullet whined by Shale's head, just missing.

'Judas Priest!' she blurted, then cussed.

'Let's go!' Brace ordered and heeled his horse into motion.

The remaining deputy ran after them,

firing shots that did no damage. They were quickly out of range.

Brace and his gang shot out of town and didn't stop riding for better than a mile before drawing up. The others gathered around him.

'Goddamn shame about June,' Shale muttered, seeing the sorrow in April and May's eyes.

'Sure didn't go the way we planned, Brace,' said Calamity Annie. 'That ain't never happened before.'

'Hope it ain't a trend.' His eye narrowed, as he gazed in the direction of town. 'Reckon we'll be visitin' again sometime soon and there'll be a bill to pay.'

'That feelin' you had, Brace, reckon that was it?' Shale looked at him with a look of concern.

He shook his head. 'Like to say it was, but I got a notion we ain't seen the last of our troubles.'

6

THE outlaw's face wavered before his vision and Steve hesitated on the trigger. The thunderous beating of wings softened and his mind reeled. His hand shook as he held the Peacemaker straight-armed.

'Can't shoot me, boy, can you?' the outlaw taunted, face twisting with a vile expression, blurring, changing. 'Can't do it, you coward!'

'Nooo,' Steve mumbled, shaking his head. A violent case of the chills shuddered through him and for an instant his vision snapped clear and he was staring into the frightened features of a woman with shiny black hair and Asian features. His eyes narrowed with disbelief.

What was happening to him? Was the outlaw really here? This was no dream; he was fully awake.

'Who . . . are you?' His voice came weak, raspy.

'My name is Sarah Cheng,' the girl answered, eyes wide.

He peered at her: the outlaw's face tried to reform and he heard the distant mocking ring of laughter. Sweat trickled down Steve's face; his whole body trembled.

The beating of wings grew distant.

He lowered the Peacemaker in fractions, knowing he'd nearly made a horrible mistake and killed an innocent woman. He felt all the strength rush from his body and collapsed. His Peacemaker dropped to the floor.

The girl caught him as he pitched forward, jamming her arm beneath his and guiding him down the hall into the parlor. She helped him to the sofa, swinging his legs up, then locating a pillow for his head.

The woman left, returning a few moments later and he was conscious of her lifting his head, pouring warm liquid into his mouth. He swallowed, the taste bitter but oddly soothing. She forced half a cupful down his throat. After, he lay back, the liquid dribbling down his chin.

The woman walked from the room again, returning moments later with a basin and cloth. She dabbed the liquid from his chin, placed the cloth over his forehead.

He took shallow ragged breaths and his consciousness flittered in and out, hazy images of Elana, the black bird and the outlaw whisking across his mind.

'Wh-where . . . am . . . I?' He struggled for words, lips gummy and tongue thick.

'Do not try to speak.' The woman placed her finger to his lips. 'You must sleep now. You will be all right.'

His eyes closed, mind wandering along dusky trails. He had no idea how long he remained in a stupor. Distantly, he was conscious of the sun rising and falling, perhaps five or six times. Images of the woman filtered in and out. When he was half-awake, she would force more of the bitter liquid into him. The pain at his shoulder lessened until it became a dull throb and on the sixth morning he awoke.

Everything looked startlingly bright and clear. Honey-gold sunlight poured through the parlor windows, and warmth flooded over his body. The chills and sweats had vanished and he felt stronger, clear-headed. He forced himself into a sitting position and peered at the shoulder wound, seeing clean cotton bandages and a sling.

As he lay back, his gaze took in the parlor. It was decorated with a subtly foreign taste, oriental. He saw various statues of Chinese origin, Buddhas and Quen Yens, pagodas and small Oriental fans on one wall; a large woven rug lay on the floor, harmonious in its color scheme with a central dragon framed by floral patterns.

The room reminded him of the woman who had nursed him back to health, changing his bandages and forcing the healing liquid down his throat.

A sound broke his reverie and he looked up to see her entering the parlor, a cup in her hands. She was a vision, he saw that now. Radiant and shimmering with sunlight, her blue-black hair touched her shoulders and accented her porcelain features; her dark eyes were bright and alert, though he thought he saw a trace of sadness there, something hidden. A Chinese gown hugged her small exquisite figure, something to behold for a man who'd been in the saddle for way too long.

'You are awake,' she said in nearly perfect English. 'I have brought you more tea but perhaps you would now prefer coffee?'

'Yes, ma'am, I surely would.'

She nodded and hurried off, returning a few moments later with a steaming cup of Arbuckle's. The brew tasted bitter yet felt immensely comforting in his belly. She brought him another cup, this time taking longer and returning with some small warm cakes. He devoured five of the cakes before she stopped him.

'Do not eat too much yet,' she said. 'It is your first day awake.'

'I'm beholden to you, ma'am. You hadn't come along, I would have died.' His gaze went to his Peacemaker, which lay on the table, and vague recollection stirred. 'Seems I owe you an apology, 'bout that, I mean.' He nodded to the gun.

'You frightened me,' she said simply, a strange darkness filtering across her eyes.

'Never meant to.'

Some of the darkness in her eyes muted. 'You were with fever. It was not your fault.'

'I thought I saw someone I'd come to find.'

Her eyes narrowed. 'You must have intended to kill this person . . . '

'Not exactly. I came to bring him to justice. If he didn't come peaceably . . . ' He let the words trail off.

128

'An outlaw?' Her eyes brightened and Steve wondered about that. She was hiding something behind her controlled rigid manner, something that saddened her.

'That's what folks hire me for, to chase down out-laws. I either turn them over to the law or put them in the ground, to put it bluntly.'

'You are what they call a bounty hunter?' She moved to the window, stared out.

'Some call it that. Others say it's legal murder. I like to think there's something a bit more noble to it.'

'Is there?' She turned, dark eyes locking with his, gaze unwavering.

'Reckon there is. I believe in what I do, ma'am. Plenty of bad folk out there, takin' things that don't belong to them, hurtin' others. Law can't always do something about it and in the West justice is greased. Too many hardcases slip out of the law's hands.'

'And that is where you come in?'

He nodded. 'That's where I come in.

But don't get me wrong, I don't like killin'. Rather they all came peaceably, but that ain't realistic. I take as big a risk of getting myself killed.' He touched the wound at his shoulder. 'It's me or them and they make the choice.'

She came over to him, placing a hand on his chest and urging him back into a lying position. She covered his legs with an Oriental quilt. 'Rest now, Mister . . . '

'Matthews, Steve Matthews.' He had little strength to resist her.

'Mr Matthews. We will talk more later, when you are stronger.'

Over the next week his strength quickly returned. The woman, who told him her name was Sarah, gave him a cup of the medical tea every day. She brought him dinners consisting of cakes and rice, meats cooked in exotic sauces, all of which he devoured eagerly with ravenous hunger. He'd never eaten Chinese cooking but he quickly developed a taste for the pungent scents and delicate flavors, as well as a respect for the intricate preparation and attention to balance. Sarah changed the bandages daily, keeping the wound clean with something she called antiseptic. He knew of infection and gangrene but had no idea of invisible things called bacteria. It struck him as silly sometimes, that there were things he couldn't see waiting to infest his flesh and make him sick, but many an Apache ritual dealt with such invisible things, spirits who hovered above tribal members, making them ill, until a shaman performed his magic, so maybe it was possible. It made little difference because the wound healed miraculously and the pain ebbed. He gained nearly full use of the arm and shoulder after just two weeks.

As dusk fell, he went to the dining area and sat himself at the table, on which she had set out a large bowl of steaming jasmine rice and steamed vegetables, plus more of the little cakes.

She poured him a cup of Arbuckle's and set the pot on the table, then poured herself tea and seated herself across from him.

'How'd you know how to fix me up?' he asked, after they'd eaten the meal in silence. He'd learned Sarah wasn't one for talking while there was food on the table, unlike his family where they jawed constantly. She ate with her head bowed, eschewing silverware in favor of fingers and two little sticks, which he had tried with no success and a great deal of frustration.

'The man who owned this house was a doctor.' The words came slow, measured and heavy with sorrow. 'I assisted him. I learned all he learned.'

'What happened to him?'

She hesitated, dark eyes dropping. 'He . . . died.'

He frowned. 'I'm sorry, ma'am.'

'It happened seven months ago. I should be over it by now.' Her voice held a certain coldness, a certain calculated resolve. She impressed him as someone who had lived through hard times, someone used to suppressing what she felt. Apaches sometimes acted in that manner.

'Some things you never get over. Lord above, that's a fact.'

'Perhaps you are right, Mr Matthews.' She stood and cleared away the dishes. He helped and after the plates were cleaned, she went to the parlor. Steve followed, sitting on the sofa. She took a Chinese lute, a *yueqin* from the corner and placed its circular body firmly in her lap. Her fingers glided over the strings, plucking with a deftness and feeling he had seldom witnessed. She told him each note played carried cosmological connotations, a deeper significance, attached to the essence of life itself. He listened, letting the tones wander through him, remembering back to his Apache origins, something spiritual stirring inside him.

Outside, a sudden cawing broke his reverie. He stood, going to the window and looking out, but he saw nothing.

The crow's call reminded him of what he had come to Wyoming to do and he felt resolve suddenly take hold. He'd almost grown lost in the peace he'd experienced recovering, being around Sarah. The serenity. She had proved moody and uncommunicative at times, but those were balanced by her lapses into elegant philosophy and medical knowledge she shared with him in the late evening hours. He could become entirely too used to living here.

You came to track the Widow Gang.

Yes, he had and he'd lost two weeks. As well, Elana would be worried, not having heard from him in over a month and a half. It was time to finish what he had begun.

He turned from the window to find Sarah staring at him. 'It follows you, Mr Matthews.' A thin smile played on her lips. 'It has been here every day since you came.'

'What?'

'The black bird, it follows you.'

He let out a thin laugh. 'It guides

me, maybe. Indians believe things like that.'

She stood, setting the lute in the corner and lacing her fingers. 'You are Indian?'

'Partly. Apache mother, white father.'

'Then you understand honor?'

'Yes, ma'am, I surely do. Even if I weren't Indian I'd understand it. It's part of what drives me to do what I do.'

'Will you do this forever, Mr Matthews?'

He wondered where this was leading, but supposed she would tell him in time.

'No, ma'am. Fact is, this is my last job. I plan on gettin' hitched soon as I finish and go back to Texas.'

'A woman is waiting for you?' Was there disappointment in her voice? He couldn't be sure.

'Her name's Elana. Reckon she's the most beautiful woman in Texas.'

'She disapproves of your work?'

Her intuitiveness surprised him. 'She does. That's why I promised her I'd

135

make this my last case. Got my heart set on findin' some land up this way and startin' a new life.'

'Then why risk all for this man you seek?' Sorrow filled her eyes and this time he pinpointed the underlying emotion: loss. That's what it was. She had suffered some great loss and it pained her to know another woman might suffer the same.

'Because it goes deeper than the risk to myself. It's a duty. He's a vicious killer and he's leadin' a gang of cutthroats bad as any I've heard tell of. They've killed plenty of folk and they'll keep killing until they're stopped. My needs gotta come after that.'

'That is very noble, Mr Matthews.' Steve caught a hint of bitterness in her voice. 'But surely there are others who could go after him?'

'S'pose there are, but like you said, I got a sense of honor and nobody has cornered them so far. How many men can I let them kill 'fore someone does?'

She peered him more deeply. 'Then you do what is called 'the right thing', Mr Matthews?'

'Try to, but I ain't no saint. And it's damned near got me killed. Elana would never forgive me if I got myself buried.'

'Did this outlaw attack you?'

'No, Indians. Arapaho, I think.'

She gave him an odd smile. 'I did not think so. Outlaws do not use arrows.'

'Not usually . . . ' He ran a finger over his upper lip, wondering about the Indians, the feeling of wrongness about the attack.

'But there have been no Indian attacks in this area for quite some time, Mr Matthews.'

He shrugged. 'Same thing occurred to me. Something struck me as odd 'bout the way they acted, way they carried themselves. Didn't strike me as Indian. And their horses, they were decked out like white men's horses.'

'Arapaho are known as expert horse

137

thieves. Perhaps that explains it.'

'Maybe, but I got a notion there's more to it than that. Ain't likely I'll ever find out, though. They're long gone.'

Sarah moved to a window and stared out into the star-sprinkled night. She appeared lost in thought and Steve wondered what she was thinking, what had made her question him. She was different than any woman he'd ever met. Perhaps some of it could be attributed to her culture, perhaps some to whatever secret saddened her. He knew little about the Chinese, only that some 30,000 of them had immigrated to America after 1850, to work in goldfields and on the railroad. The Orientals worked for low pay and accepted harsh slave treatment no white man ever would. But this quickly elicited anti-Chinese sentiment among many whites, along with the vast cultural and religious differences. Being half-breed, Steve had experienced much the same thing.

'The fella who died, ma'am, he your husband?' Steve asked, breaking the silence. He felt the sudden urge to know more about Sarah, her hidden sadness, and the feeling disturbed him.

'No, he was not, Mr Matthews. Does that make you think less of me?' A challenge edged her voice; he knew she had faced the criticism before and it hurt her.

'I'm part Apache, ma'am. Most white men wouldn't understand the ways of my tribe, so I figure I got no right to judge the ways of others.'

'Thank you, Mr Matthews.'

'He brought you here?'

'Yes. He purchased me from my owner.'

'He bought you?' Surprise crossed his face.

'Do not think wrongly of him, Mr Matthews. He was a kind man. He saw me working as a slave in Chinatown and purchased me from my owner, then offered me freedom, but I chose to stay with him. I loved him and

139

he loved me. We needed nothing else between us.'

Steve smiled. 'Must have been a hell of a man.'

'He was that, Mr Matthews. He died because of it.'

'Wish you'd call me Steve, ma'am.'

'Steve, then. But you must call me Sarah.' He nodded and she paused, the sorrow in her eyes darkening to muted anger. He saw she had her mind set on something and he got the notion he would soon find out where all her questions had been leading.

'You have told me this man you seek was to be your last job, but I have a favor to ask you.'

'Name it. I owe you plenty for what you done for me.'

'I want you to find someone for me.'

His brow crinkled and he didn't like the feeling he was suddenly getting. 'Who?'

'I told you the man who owned this house died; I should have told you he was murdered.'

Steve's belly sank. 'Murdered? By an outlaw?'

'Yes, by an outlaw, as you call him. I call him a devil.'

'Why? You have nothing an outlaw'd want.'

Her eyes glossed with tears. 'Jason, that was his name, treated a man who had been shot, a man in a mask. When he was finished, that man killed him. I was standing next to Jason when it happened. I held him as he died.'

'You were a witness and he let you live?' Incredible as that seemed to Steve, it gave him a sinking feeling. One man was known for that and one man alone.

'He told me he would not kill me. Many times I wish he had.'

Though he knew the answer, he asked, 'If this man was wearing a mask, how would you recognise him again?'

'He had one eye, Mr . . . *Steve*.'

Shock welded onto Steve's face. One eye. The Widow Maker! No one else

141

fitted that description.

'You look surprised,' Sarah said.

Steve's gaze locked with hers. 'This man, he have a gang of women with him?'

'Women?' She shook her head. 'No, he was alone.'

'S'pose he might have left them somewhere and come for treatment himself not knowing what he'd walk into.'

'Do you know this man?' He caught a note of hope in her voice.

Hesitating, he licked his lips. The man known as the Widow Maker had suddenly taken on a personal edge — he was responsible for the sadness in Sarah's eyes and that angered Steve more than he cared to admit. 'I came to find me a man with one eye who wears a mask. A man they call the Widow Maker. He don't kill womenfolk, just men. He held up a stage in this area seven months ago. Sure sounds like the same hombre who killed your man.'

Her eyes widened with hope. 'Then

142

you will help me?'

'If he's the man I came to find, you don't even need to ask.'

'I have one more request, Steve.' She gave him a cold smile and he didn't like the feeling he got from it.

'Like I said, I owe you plenty.'

'I wish to accompany you.'

'Now wait a — '

'He murdered the man I loved. I wish to see him die.'

'Chasin' outlaws is no job for a woman,' was all he managed to get out and he knew it was lame.

She folded her arms. 'He travels with women.'

'That's true, but he's a vicious killer. I planned to pick me up a marshal and some deputies, form a posse. You'd stand a high chance of being killed.'

'I know how to use a gun.'

He eyed her, a frown turning his lips. Her decision was made; he saw it would be impossible to change her mind. But how could he let her risk her life? The choice was not his, that was plain; it was hers. Admiration for the woman filled him. He respected her strength; she had the soul of an Apache.

He sighed in resignation. 'Ain't likely I can talk you out of this, is it?'

'You could no sooner convince a dragon not to breathe flame.'

He had notion she was right. 'I don't like it one bit.'

She gave him a wafer smile. 'Do not worry, Steve. You said this man does not kill women.'

'There's always a first time . . . '

* * *

The next morning Sarah took him to the small stable beside the house, where they hitched a buckboard to a thickly muscled horse Jason Parker had used to make rounds and attend to housecalls in Deadeye. In order to resume his search for the Widow Gang he would need to replenish his supplies, acquire fresh horses. His ammunition was running low and he'd need another Winchester.

Sarah had changed into riding clothes and kept silent most of the way to town. He saw darkness behind her eyes, a mixture of sorrow and grim determination. She saw vengeance approaching, the conclusion to something that had started seven months ago — the desire for retribution. Steve had tried to make her reconsider over breakfast but she would have none of it. Her mind was set and only the death of the one-eyed outlaw could appease the burning lust for justice inside her. Steve understood her feelings but wished he could somehow shield her from them. When the Widow Maker died, her pain would not end and killing a man changed something within you. It hardened you, stayed in your mind, a pocket of poison.

They rode into Deadeye about half past ten, rattling to a halt in front of the general store. A telegraph office stood beside it, his first destination.

He climbed from the seat and entered the office, operator glancing up and slapping slips of paper on the counter. He sent two telegrams while Sarah waited beside him, dark eyes curious but distant. The operator cast her an occasional glance that held some hidden meaning but said nothing. The first telegram went to a Ranger friend of his in Texas, asking for any new information on the whereabouts of the gang, as well as reports of any renegade Indian attacks in the Wyoming area. The second went to Elana, informing her that he was all right and the case would take a little longer than he planned. She would still be worried but the telegraph would help and at least she would know he was alive.

As they left the office and walked out on to the boardwalk, the operator's gaze followed them.

Steve glanced at Sarah. 'That fella, he got some kind of bug in his britches?'

She gave a humorless smile. 'There

146

is much anti-Chinese sentiment in Deadeye. It is a small town. I cannot even buy supplies at the general store.'

Shock welded on to his face. 'What? How do you survive?'

'The marshal befriended Jason. He likes me and brings me supplies, which I pay for by mending and doing cleaning for him. He is alone and needs the help.'

'Judas Priest!' Steve shook his head. He had encountered some of the same attitudes himself, men who didn't cotton to Indians in general and half-breeds in particular: He reckoned it would be much the same for her, though more difficult because she was woman in a man's West. She would not be able to overcome prejudice with her fists or a Peacemaker.

'Well, we're gonna need supplies at the general store and the gun shop. Reckon someone's gonna sell them to me or there'll be hell to pay.'

A distressed look crossed her face. 'It

will not be so easy, Steve. I am Chinese you are half-Indian. The store owner is a small man.'

'He'll be smaller by the time I get done with him.' Steve strode into the general store with a spur of irritation under his skin. The store was gloomy, with dusty shafts of light spilling across worn floorboards. He scanned the rows of supplies — canned goods, bottles of potions for an assortment of ailments, sacks of grain — for what he needed.

Upon seeing them walk in, the owner stiffened and gave him a look blatant in its intent.

'You best not bother, mister. I don't sell to no Chinawoman or Injuns.' The man kept his hands poised on the edge of the counter; Steve reckoned he likely had a shotgun beneath. Sizing up the fellow he recognised that glint of unreasonable hatred in his eyes. He was the type who held no regard or respect for life other than what he considered pure breeding. He would kill either of them given the provocation, but it would take a good push, shooting only if forced into it. If Steve knew the type, there was also a measure of yellow, but he would take no chances. He couldn't afford to have the situation turn ugly.

He glanced at Sarah, who appeared unperturbed by the statement.

His Peacemaker cleared leather in a blur of motion and the owner's face dropped, a sudden fearful respect for the young man before him flashing in his eyes. His hands never had the chance to lift from the counter and go for the rifle.

'You're robbin' me?' Shock hit the 'keep's face, along with fear.

'No, sir, I'm not. We need supplies and I ain't got time to argue prejudice with you.' He motioned to Sarah, who began selecting the supplies they needed. 'You'll be paid well for your stock, but if you got any notions of going for the shotgun beneath your counter, you best forget 'em, now.'

The man's eyes narrowed, hate glittering in them like twin devils.

Steve stifled a satisfied smile, knowing technically what he was doing was not the most diplomatic way to handle the situation, but deciding he had no time to discuss options.

Sarah finished gathering supplies and loaded them onto the buckboard. Steve fished a roll of greenbacks from his pocket and peeled off enough bills to cover the supplies plus an extra five dollars.

He backed out of the store, making sure the owner didn't take the notion to fill his backside with buckshot, and closed the door.

'Bet he'll be steamin' for a spell.' Steve climbed into the seat beside Sarah. She gave him a smile that actually held some warmth.

'He may get the marshal.'

Steve grinned. 'Marshal's a friend of yours, ain't he?'

'Yes.' Her smile widened and he snapped the reins. The buckboard rattled into motion, bouncing along the rutted street until they reached the gun shop. Pulling up in front, they climbed down and entered the shop, which was somewhat brighter and cleaner than the general store. Steve noticed two men leaning against the far end of the counter, each puffing a smoke, eyeing him and Sarah. The proprietor, who fiddled with a gunstock behind the counter, looked up as they approached, gaze narrowing.

'He'p ya?' he asked, brow crinkling, bushy grey brows almost hiding his dull green eyes.

Steve nodded, throwing a glance at the two other men, who seemed particularly interested in Sarah. He felt that sudden sixth sense tingle through him, warning him he'd best watch his back.

'I need a Winchester. Spare shells for it and my Peacemaker.'

The owner eyed him. 'You half-Injun?'

Steve tensed. 'Yeah, what of it?'

'She Chinese?' He nudged his head towards Sarah.

'Make your point, fella.' Steve tensed, ready to use Peacemaker persuasion again, but hoping he wouldn't have to.

The gunsmith shrugged. 'S'pose it don't matter a lick to me. Just don't want trouble.'

'We ain't looking for none.'

'You an outlaw?'

'Nope, bounty hunter.'

The man's face softened. 'Who you after?'

'Man called the Widow Maker.'

The shopkeep's eyes widened. A shocked look crossed his face. 'You best talk to the deputy about that.'

'Why? And why not the marshal?'

'Marshal's dead.' The man turned and began filling Steve's order.

Sarah's face went white and her body trembled, then deep sadness clouded her eyes. Steve let out a long sigh.

'He was a fine man, Steve,' she said, as he touched her shoulder. He saw tears gather behind her eyes but they didn't flow.

The 'keep finished setting a Winchester .44-40 on the counter, along with two boxes of shells. Steve plucked a number of greenbacks from his roll and tossed them down.

'What happened?' he asked the gunsmith. 'It involve the gang I'm after?'

The 'keep shook his head. 'Like I said, talk to the deputy.'

'I'll just do that.' Steve scooped up the rifle and passed the boxes of shells to Sarah. 'Much obliged.'

'Don't advertise it,' said the man solemnly.

For the moment Steve had lost interest in the men at the end of the counter. That was a mistake. They had manoeuvred behind him and Sarah, and as Steve turned one man held out a hand, thumping it against his chest. He saw a demon of intent in the man's eyes.

'You shouldn't be sellin' to no Injuns and Chinagirls,' the man said, casting the shopkeeper an icy look.

'Now, you just hold on one god-damned minute, Jake!' The 'keep looked indignant. 'You and Bart got no right tellin' me who I can sell to. This here's my store.'

'I got every right,' the man called Jake said. 'We don't need no heathens in this town. We got plenty of dirt already.'

Steve's face went red and without deliberation he jerked the Winchester up, bringing it around the man's outstretched arm. The stock took the man square in the side of the head; a stream of blood rushed down his face.

'Christamighty!' he roared, instinctively winging a gloved fist at Steve. The man was half-stunned, the punch delivered in a sloppy manner and Steve ducked easily. He swung the rifle again in a short arc, clouting the man in the jaw with the butt.

The man staggered backward but before Steve could exploit the opportunity, the one called Bart swung a fist that caught him on the temple.

Steve's head whirled and he dropped the Winchester. The man, who out-weighed him by fifty pounds, hit him again. Distantly he heard Sarah yell, as she tried to stop the man, but Jake, partially recovered, grabbed her, clamping a hand over her mouth.

Steve tried to get up a protective arm, but didn't succeed. The attacker was strong and fast and Steve had not completely recovered from the arrow wound. The man's fist bounced from Steve's jaw and his senses went south. The floor rushed up to meet him.

The attacker leaped atop him, grabbing a handful of his hair, poising to slam his face into the hoards.

The scritch of a hammer being drawn back suddenly stopped him. He let go of Steve's hair and climbed off, backing against the counter.

It took Steve a moment to orient himself, stop his head from spinning. When he reached his feet, he saw a deputy standing just inside the door, leveling a Peacemaker.

'Let her go,' the deputy said, nudging his gun at the man holding Sarah. Jake released her and stepped away.

'Hell, we was just funnin', Deputy,' Jake said. 'No need to get riled over it.'

The deputy's face turned grim. 'We got enough trouble in this town, Jake. We don't want no more. Get out.'

Jake's eyes narrowed and he flashed Steve a look, then brushed past the deputy, disappearing outside. The other fellow grunted and followed him out.

'Sorry, 'bout that, Miss Cheng.' The deputy holstered his Peacemaker. 'Not all the folk in Deadeye got a brain, as you well know.'

'I am very thankful, Deputy.' She gave a slight bow.

Steve retrieved his Winchester and the deputy came over to him, extending a hand.

'Deputy Peterson,' he said.

'Steve Matthews.'

'General store owner came to me

with a complaint 'bout you, Mr Matthews. Said you kept him at gunpoint while you took supplies. I saw your buckboard outside and decided I'd ask you about it. Good thing I did.'

'Am I in trouble for that?' Steve asked, knowing his methods fell somewhere south of legal sometimes.

'Said you paid, plus extra, so I reckon it ain't robbery.' The deputy seemed to consider it. 'Mr Tidly could use a good scare. Hell, maybe this will put the fear of God into him, but I doubt it. Hate dies hard.'

'Thanks, Deputy. Reckon I didn't see no other way.'

'Tell him about the killin's, Deputy,' said the store owner. Steve saw a note of fear in the 'keep's eyes.

'Who are you, Mr Matthews, if you don't mind my askin'?'

'I'm a manhunter. I came to track down the Widow Gang. Miss Cheng says they killed the doc here seven months back.'

The deputy nodded. 'That they did, and a week ago they killed the marshal, along with three deputies. Shot up the saloon somethin' awful. I was figurin' on gathering a posse to go after them, but not many a man wants a part of them. They left fear in this town, Mr Matthews.'

Steve pondered it a moment. 'Then they're likely riding South — that's where the next town is. Consider yourself with posse, now, Deputy. Miss Cheng and I are going after them and there's no reason we can't join up with you.'

The deputy eyed Sarah and a dim doubt crossed his face, but he said nothing. 'We'd best wait.'

'Why?' Steve leaned against the counter, rubbing his temple, which throbbed from the blow.

'Two days from now a stage will be transporting some gold from Colorado way, same one that rode through seven months ago. Reckon it will be too tempting for them to pass up. They got balls, Mr Matthews — pardon me, ma'am' — he tipped his hat to Sarah, who smiled — 'and won't think twice 'bout hittin' it again. I got a notion to be waitin' on them — if I find me enough men.'

Steve thought it over. A surprise attack. That would even the odds, lessen the risk to Sarah.

Steve nodded. 'Reckon we'll meet you day after tomorrow to go over details, then. 'Bout dawn?'

The deputy looked grim. ''Bout dawn, Mr Matthews. But I suggest you leave the lady home. Hate to see anything worse happen to her.'

Steve gave a brittle smile. 'Convincing her of that would be tougher than fighting the gang.'

'Thought as much.' The deputy smiled and tipped his hat to Sarah, then walked out of the shop.

7

DESPITE the incident in town the day hadn't been a loss for Steve Matthews. He had stumbled across a lead to the Widow Gang and signed on with the deputy to bring the bandits to justice.

Before leaving town, Steve had purchased two strong horses, trailing them behind the buckboard back to the house. On the ride back Sarah remained quiet, sombre, lost in thought. He reckoned she was dwelling on her loss, and on the outlaw who had killed her loved one. If all went well, she would have her revenge in two days, and that always brought a certain sting of remorse. When the Widow Maker died, she would have nothing but memories to hold on to. The hope of finding the killer had given her purpose, a diversion in a sense. He knew that tenuous thread held some folks to their lives; he hoped it wasn't so with Sarah. She was a strong woman but everyone had a breaking point and the need to see justice, no, *retribution* carried out might be all that kept her from stepping over the line. He had seen it before, in the faces of women who'd hired him to track the killer of a loved one. When he brought them the news justice had been served he saw the look, a strange look, one of curious elation tinged with hollowness. He had watched all life wash out of them at that instant of fulfilled vengeance. Perhaps it had been gone already, merely a granted reprieve, a marionette with its string suddenly clipped.

As he entered the parlor, hands wrapped about a cup of coffee, he peered at the Chinese woman, who stood by the window, gazing out into the dying day. It occurred to him she faced something worse than loneliness. She could be killed in the ambush of the gang. That was something he doubted he could live with.

He cleared his throat. 'Wish I could say something that would make you forget about goin' with us, Sarah.'

She turned, face grave, betraying a memory that haunted her. 'You cannot, Steve. I will see that man punished for what he did.'

Steve sighed. 'He'll be punished. I just hope you got something left after he does.'

She gave him an unreadable look then went to the corner and lifted the *yueqin*. Sitting, she began to pluck sombre elegant tones, growing lost in some other world, a shrouded world of sorrow and tears, ghosts of the past. He listened, growing lost himself, a curious sense of peace washing over him.

A jangling crash shattered the serenity. He jolted, heart leaping. Shards of glass rained to the carpet as the window disintegrated. An arrow shrieked past him, barely missing, and embedded itself into the sofa. A series of yips and yowls followed, hoofbeats.

Steve set his cup on the table, gaze snapping to the window. Sarah, startled, laid the *yueqin* against the wall and rose.

Steve went to the window, keeping to the side and chancing a look outside. His gaze swept the front yard.

'The Indians!' he muttered, amazed.

'How did they find you?' asked Sarah, vague worry on her face.

'Reckon it wouldn't be too difficult to follow the trail I left but the question is why bother? Can't see them wanting to attack this close to town.'

He slid his Peacemaker from its holster as one of the Indians veered right. He triggered a shot, plucking the fellow from the saddle. To say he was amazed would have been an understatement. Indians were as at home on horses as white men were on the ground. That one would foolishly make himself an easy target was befuddling.

He shook his head. 'This don't make sense,' he said to no one in particular, as his gaze shifted to the other riders. Three remained, but before he could draw a bead on the next, Sarah rushed to the other window and, heaving it up a few inches, jammed a Winchester through the slot. She levered a shell into the chamber and squeezed the trigger. An Indian screeched, the sound blood-curdling, almost girlish. He flew backwards off his horse, slamming into the dirt, unmoving.

The remaining two braves had forked off, leaping from their mounts. One scurried behind the huge bole of a cottonwood while the other ran to a rain barrel, ducking behind it. The man was carrying something, but Steve couldn't tell what. Steve fired; lead punched a hole in the barrel and an arcing stream of water spouted out.

In retaliation, another arrow hurtled towards the window. It thunked into the side of the house, rattling. Sarah triggered another shot, missing.

The situation puzzled him no end. He never expected the Indians to track him this far just to settle a score. He suspected they'd merely wanted his horse and supplies. Those being long gone, they would simply lie in wait for their next victim. *If* they were renegade Arapaho. But Indian or not, the attackers were after him for a reason, one that went beyond simple Indian highjinks.

'Two of them, two of us.' Steve glanced at the Chinese girl. 'Even odds, I'd say.'

She nodded, brow crinkling. 'They are not Indians.'

'What?' His eyes widened as she confirmed what he'd been thinking. 'How can you tell at this distance?'

Sarah never got the chance to answer because an arrow whisked through the window, aflame. It ploughed into the Oriental tapestry on the opposite wall. Steve dived for it, ripping the tapestry from the wall and smothering the flames. Another flaming arrow whipped through the window, embedding itself into a chair. The material caught, snakes of flame dancing up.

Two more arrows sailed into the brush next to the house. Dry leaves crackled as flame gobbled them, musky smoke rising in clouds.

Sarah jumped from the window and snatched the blanket from the sofa, throwing it over the burning chair. Plumes of smoke billowed from beneath.

An explosive *whoof*! ripped out and Steve's belly plunged. He knew that sound.

'Kerosene!' he shouted, as Sarah shot him a frightened look. Now he knew what the man had been carrying. 'You're right about them not bein' Indians. Whoever heard of Indians attacking with kerosene?'

The arrows entering the parlor had diverted Steve and Sarah just long enough for one of the Indians to creep close enough to the house to douse a wall with kerosene, then set it aflame. The man had scurried back to cover by the time Steve reached the window.

Black smoke tumbled across the yard, blackening the already dimming day. Flames lapped the house, devouring dry wood. Inside, the heat grew intense.

Sarah rushed to the window and fired two quick shots, hitting nothing. Another flaming arrow whined through the window, striking the sofa. Flame danced across the cushions and smoke clogged the room.

'We don't get out we're done for!' Steve's voice cracked above the crepitation of flame. He moved away from the window, coughing, smoke choking his lungs.

'As soon as we step out they'll kill us!' Sarah backed from the window.

A grim look crossed his face. 'Go out the back! Don't stop running 'til you reach town. There's only two left. I'll go out the front and divert their attention.'

'They will kill you!' Panic laced her voice, one of the few times he'd heard such emotion in her tone.

'That's what they came here for. I

don't know why, but that was their aim all along. You're not involved. I can take care of myself, don't worry.' He lied. He carried no illusions as to what would happen when he went out that door. They would be waiting for just that move and he would be a dead man. But he wanted Sarah safe at all costs and would accept his fate. He had brought these men here and he alone would take responsibility for it.

Seeing her hesitation, he leaped forward and shoved her towards the kitchen. He had no time to argue with her. Flames skirted the windows now and the entire sofa was alight. Stressed beams snapped, creaked, groaned. Within moments supports would start to give; shortly after the place would collapse. Long before that the smoke would kill them.

She shot him a defiant look, but went towards the back, keeping her Winchester ready. He got the disturbing notion she wouldn't heed his advice and instead circle the house and try to help him. He hoped he was wrong.

Steve crossed the parlor, reaching the front door. Thick black smoke stung his eyes and a series of racking coughs rattled his chest. He threw the door open and plunged outside, Peacemaker up, finger on the trigger.

He came out at an angle, diving sideways, partially engulfed in plumes of smoke. He hoped to gain himself a few extra seconds of life, mount a defence. Through watery, blurry vision he spotted an Indian stepping from behind the barrel and coming straight at him.

A shot blasted from the back of the house and with sudden horror he realised one of the attackers had circled to the back, not knowing which way he'd come out.

His blood ran cold as he thought about Sarah.

The Indian stopped and lifted his bow. He aimed at Steve's chest, drawing back.

Steve tried to get his Peacemaker to

aim but he could only see a wavy blurred figure.

The Indian suddenly swung around. Steve, turning his head, saw why. Sarah had rounded the corner of the house and was levering a shell into the Winchester's chamber.

The Indian had his bow set. Sarah would not be able to aim in time.

Steve, aiming hastily, triggered his Peacemaker, praying he'd hit something, anything, divert the man's attention and throw off his aim. He got lucky. The bullet skimmed the man's leg as he released the arrow.

The arrow ploughed into the ground at Sarah's feet. He uttered a curse and went for the gun at his hip.

She got the rifle up and jerked a shot. A starburst of crimson appeared on the man's side. Shock hit his face and he dropped the bow, then crumpled to the ground, gasping. The man still lived, but would not last more than a few minutes from the looks of the wound.

Steve ran forward, holstering his

Peacemaker, gaze swinging to the house, now completely enveloped in flame.

He looked at Sarah, who stared at the flames, deep loss in her eyes.

'Where's the other one?' He laid a gentle hand on her shoulder.

'Dead. He came at me when I stepped out but I had seen him though the window. I was ready for him.'

'I'm sorry.' Steve nodded towards the house.

'It was the only thing I had left . . .' Bitterness filled her voice. A tear slipped from her eye, mixing with soot and streaking black down her face.

With a dying roar the roof caved, splashing the air with a shower of sparks. Great clouds of black smoke tumbled into the darkening sky.

Steve drew Sarah into his arms, holding her for long moments. He wished he could do more. She was used to loss and he felt infinitely sorry for her. She had nothing left, except a consuming desire to see the outlaw responsible for killing her man punished, and soon that would be taken from her as well. Steve made a decision then: if she wanted to go, he would take her back to Texas with him, have Elana help her in some way.

The fallen Indian groaned and Steve went to him, kneeling. The man wasn't Indian at all. Beneath the paint were the dark features of a Mex. A black wig hung askew on his head. Even the clothing looked wrong at close range.

'You're done for, fella.' Steve's voice held no sympathy, but a heaviness burdened his heart. 'Say your piece now 'fore the devil takes his due.'

The man peered up at him through bloodshot, teary eyes. '*Madre de Dios*,' he mumbled, lips sticky and blood-specked. A snake of blood slithered from his mouth.

'Who sent you after me?'

'Got . . . Gonzal . . . '

'*Gonzales*?' The name rang in Steve's mind, a name he reckoned he'd never again hear.

172

'He . . . he said to make it look . . . like Injuns . . . '

The man gurgled something further, then his head fell back, eyelids fluttering.

Steve stood, gaze going to Sarah, who looked at him with sorrow and confusion.

Steve's words came low, grim. 'Gonzales. My last case. I brought him in for robbin' a bank in Matadero. Reckon he had friends and an itch to get even. I'd best send a wire and see if he's still in jail.'

She nodded and they went towards the barn. There was nothing further they could do here. The house was burning itself out, occasional snaps and crackles sending sparks of flame into the dusk. He wouldn't bother to bury the dead man. He'd inform the law when they got to town and the undertaker could take care of it. Saddling the horses, they mounted and rode for Deadeye, trailing the animal who had pulled the buckboard behind. They would board him at the livery.

173

When they reached town they drew up in front of the deputy's office. Steve's features were set in grim lines and Sarah's face had drawn tight, emotionless.

As they entered, the deputy turned from where he was standing at a small table, pouring coffee into a tin cup.

His brow raised. 'Mr Matthews, Miss Cheng. Didn't expect to see you 'til mornin' after next.'

Steve nodded and Sarah remained silent. He guided her to a chair. 'Some hardcases burned down the house. They dressed up to make it look like Indians done it.'

The deputy's face darkened. 'What were they after?'

Steve's lips drew tight. 'Me. They were hired by a man I put in jail. He wanted to get even.'

'They dead?'

Steve nodded.

The deputy poured two more tin cups of coffee and handed one to Sarah, one to Steve.

174

Steve nudged his head towards Sarah. 'She's been through a hell of a time, Deputy.' Steve sat in a hard-backed chair as the deputy moved around his desk and lowered himself into a seat.

'You're welcome to stay here. Got those cots in the cells. Ain't the most comfortable — '

'That will be fine,' Sarah cut in. 'Thank you for your kindness.'

The deputy gave her a thin smile. 'Ain't nothin', ma'am. Wish I could do better.'

Steve cocked an eyebrow. 'There's a hotel — '

'It will not cater to Chinese or Indians,' Sarah said briskly. 'I have no strength to argue with them.'

Steve did, but he had no desire to put her through further hardship.

'Since you're here, Mr Matthews, reckon we can go over those plans now.'

Steve nodded, taking a sip of coffee. The deputy opened a desk drawer and pulled out a rolled-up tube of paper.

He spread it out, setting his cup on one corner and his Peacemaker on another. It was a map showing an area of terrain marked with Xs at various spots.

The deputy stabbed a finger at the map. 'Closest town to Deadeye is a three-day ride south. Reckon those *hombres* have camped somewhere in between. Reckon they'll know about the stage. Counting on it, anyway. They knew 'bout the one seven months ago.'

'Stage only come through once every seven months?' Steve asked.

'No, comes through once a week, but only once or twice a year does it carry a gold shipment. Man named Stalwright up in Montana owns a gold mine down Colorado way. Has a shipment transferred when he runs low on cash. 'Course the last was a loss so he immediately had another shipped up. Bandits missed that one 'cause it was so close. Doubt they'll miss this one.'

'So this is where you think they'll

strike?' He pointed to a spot marked with an X.

'I do, Mr Matthews. The terrain is the most diverse there. Easiest place to get a jump on the stage.'

'How many men you got?'

The deputy's gaze dropped to the map, came back up. 'One so far.'

Steve sighed and shook his head. 'With Sarah and me that'll make four. Against the likes of that gang that's not four aces, even with a surprise attack.'

'There'll be two drivers and two hired guns in the stage. That should do it.'

Steve nodded. 'That makes things better, though it didn't help much last time.'

'No, it didn't. But they got the jump on them. This time the tables will be turned.'

As the deputy rolled up the map, Steve stood, a sudden dread washing through his being. The sensation of apprehension plagued him for no reason he could think of. Everything looked to be to their advantage. 'You sure these *hombres* would risk hitting this close to Deadeye after shootin' up the town?'

'I do, Mr Matthews. They got nothin' to fear. They know the town has only one deputy left. They figure no one would be foolish enough to come after them. We killed one of their own and saw their faces. After they hit the stage I got me no doubts they'll be back to settle up with me.'

Steve nodded. 'They didn't reckon I'd be doggin' 'em, though.'

'That's what I'm countin' on, Mr Matthews.'

After asking the deputy to watch over Sarah, Steve strolled out into the evening. He led the big bay Sarah used to pull the buckboard towards the livery. He thought over the deputy's plan to put an end to the Widow Maker's rampages. The lawman had gumption. After the devastating loss to Deadeye most would have crawled under a rock, but the fellow was going right after the bandits.

On the surface the plan looked good: seven men and one woman against one man and five women, by surprise attack. Better odds than he normally worked with.

So why did he feel an odd sensation of doom stalking him? Did the nightmares involving the outlaw and Elana and great black bird have anything to do with it? Was it the thought of Sarah risking death at the hands of the gang? By all standards he should be confident. But he was not.

A cawing pulled him from his thoughts. He looked up to see the crow perched on the uppermost lip of a false front. The bird stared at him with glassy black eyes. A hint of a chill went down his spine. He shook it off, hoping it wasn't a bad omen.

He stepped off the boardwalk and crossed to the livery. Leading the horse inside, he searched for the owner, not finding him. After guiding the horse into a stall, he checked the small back room that served as an office. The room was empty and Steve assumed the attendant had stepped out for supper. He'd visit the café and check, but would first wait a few moments to give the fellow time to finish his grub. He leaned against a stall, the smell of leather, hay and dung musky in his nostrils. Horses nickered.

The Widow Gang: Would they chance coming back as the deputy thought they would? Steve had to agree it sounded logical. Deadeye had been left virtually defenceless and one of the gang's own lay in the local cemetery. But that would come after they got the gold and Steve agreed with the lawman's assessment the stage would be too tempting to such a band of cutthroats. If they knew about the shipment. They had the first, so it was safe to assume they did.

He wondered about the women in the gang. That was a new angle. He'd never shot a woman, let alone killed one. That gave him pause. They were cold-blooded killers, he reminded himself, dangerous as any man. He had no choice. They would not hesitate to kill him. He'd make certain to keep that in mind when the time came.

A scuffing sound from behind caught his attention and he started to turn, thinking it was the livery man.

Something collided with the back of his head. He staggered forward, a warm stream of blood streaking down the side of his face. The livery whirled and horses whinnied, stamped, suddenly spooked, as he slammed into a stall door.

A laugh rang out, mocking and humorless. He turned his head, seeing the two men who had attacked him in the gun shop earlier standing behind him. The one called Bart had a gun out, leveled at his chest, and the other, Jake, grabbed a pitchfork.

'Looks like you ain't got no one here to save you this time, Injun boy,' Jake grinned. 'This town don't need your heathen type. You shoulda took our warnin' and left.'

'You go to hell!' Steve snapped without thinking and the man got a furious glint in his eyes. He jabbed the pitchfork at him and Steve jerked back, barely avoiding being skewered.

The men meant business. Earlier they had been disgraced by the deputy and now they would take their revenge on Steve. In the gun shop encounter, Steve reckoned they merely intended to put hurt on him, send him running from town in fear. Now things had changed. They were out for blood.

Jake taunted him with jabs of the pitchfork. 'Where's your Chinawoman, Injun? Maybe we oughta pay her a visit after we finish with you.'

The other man chuckled and Steve could smell whiskey on their breath. They were half drunk, inflamed by their hate. He had few options. If he went for his gun, he could take out the one with the pitchfork, but the other would gun him down in the next instant.

Steve's gaze darted to a shovel standing against the stall door, about five feet away. Without hesitation he lunged for it.

'Hey!' Bart shouted. Jake took a step forward.

Steve snatched up the shovel and swung it around, just in time to counter a thrust of the pitchfork. Metal clanged against metal. He deflected the blow, but the man reset himself for another thrust, wavering slightly, off balance.

Stepping sideways, Steve brought the shovel up in a short arc. He thwacked Bart's gun hand with the sharp edge. The move surprised Bart, who was transfixed by the battle between Steve and Jake. The gun flew from the attacker's hand, skidding across the hay-strewn boards. Bart let out a squawk and clutched his hand.

Steve whirled to avoid another thrust of the pitchfork that would have pierced his vitals.

The momentum of the missed thrust sent the man stumbling forward and he crashed into a stall. Steve clouted him with a hammer fist to the side of the head.

He swiped a hand across his own eyes, blood dribbling in and obscuring his vision.

Bart recovered from his shock and rushed him, wrapping his arms about Steve's waist and hurling him to the aisle floor.

Steve slammed into the boards, wind exploding from his lungs. A dull pain stabbed his wounded shoulder.

With a bootheel, Bart tried to stomp Steve's head into the floor. Steve jerked left and the blow missed.

Bart followed up by jumping atop Steve's chest and using his knees to pin Steve's arms to the floor. Steve brought his legs up, locking them about the man's neck and yanking him backward.

The attacker hit the floor with a crash. Steve rolled, tried to gain hands and knees, but a boot toe connected with his jaw, snapping his teeth together and sending a shock wave of pain through his face.

Dazed, he felt himself lifted by both men and shoved against a stall. One buried a fist in his belly. Bile rose sour and burning in his throat.

He was defenceless. A few more blows would easily finish him.

A distant *clack* caught his attention — the sound of a shell being levered into a chamber. A thunderous shot halted the attack abruptly. He looked towards the door. Through blurred vision he saw Sarah and the deputy standing in the opening, Winchester in the Chinese woman's hand, Peacemaker in the deputy's, both leveled on Jake and Bart. Fire burned in her eyes. She had fired the shot. The man called Bart clutched at his thigh, blood streaming between his fingers.

'You are lucky I do not kill you.' Her voice was cold, deadly serious. Jake said nothing, sweat trickling down his face. Bart stared at her, gasping.

Jake released Steve and stepped back. The deputy motioned with his Peacemaker.

'Miss Cheng thought you'd been gone too long, Mr Matthews. She decided to come lookin' for you. Couldn't let her go out alone after all that's happened.'

'Why you takin' for the Injun and Chinagirl, Deputy?' asked Jake, sneering. 'Ain't you had enough trouble in this town lately? You gotta clean out the bad blood.'

'I aim to, Jake. And I'm startin' with you and your partner. I see either of you in this town after tonight I'll shoot you on sight. That clear?' The deputy's eyes narrowed. He meant the threat.

Jake spat but slowly nodded. He stepped over to his partner and helped him limp from the livery.

'Leave your gun,' the deputy ordered.

'Aw, Christ,' Jake muttered but his hand started for his gun.

'Slowly!' The deputy gestured with his Peacemaker. Jake edged the gun from its holster and dropped it to the floor. His partner's gun was already lying on the boards. They disappeared into the encroaching night.

'Seems like you're always savin' my life,' Steve said, as Sarah came towards him. She took his arm and helped him towards the door.

She gave him a warm smile. 'You saved mine earlier today.'

Steve let out a scoffing laugh. 'I brought on the attack, so that ain't sayin' much.'

They returned to the office and while the deputy fixed two cots for them in the cells, Sarah cleaned the blood from Steve's face and hair. The deputy finished up by hanging a blanket between the cells to give them privacy.

'Sorry, ma'am, it's the best I can do,' he told Sarah, who smiled.

'It will be fine, Deputy. Thank you.'

'Reckon I'll see you in the mornin', then.' He tipped his hat and took a bunk in the end cell, lowering the lamp flame and placing his hat over his face.

Steve looked at Sarah. In the dim light she looked lovely and the thought passed his mind that if he hadn't fallen in love with Elana he could easily grow to love this woman.

Maybe he already had.

8

SHAFTS of sunlight streamed through the barred windows and dust danced pirouettes within. Steve rose with the dawn, eager to get to the telegraph office and see whether there had been a response to his telegram to Elana. He would wire his Ranger friend again, this time about Gonzales. He intended to repay the hardcase for hiring those men to kill him. More so, he would make him pay for the pain and loss they caused Sarah. Had the hardcase escaped? Or had he directed the attack from his cell? The telegram would confirm that. If Gonzales were on the loose, well, that would mean another 'one last job' but Elana would have to understand. He owed Sarah and himself that much.

The deputy had coffee brewing by the time Steve washed up. Sarah sat

189

on the edge of her bunk, peering at them. He doubted she had slept much. He downed a quick cup of Arbuckle's, intending to take her to the café for a breakfast of steak and eggs. With the mood he was in, he pitied the next fella who didn't want to serve a half-breed and Chinese.

As they headed for the door the deputy said, 'You best watch your back case them two didn't leave town, Mr Matthews.'

Steve nodded. 'I'll keep an eye out.'

They walked along the boardwalk, the crisp morning air sweet and refreshing with the scents of autumn. The sun shone brassy in a crystal-blue sky.

Reaching the telegraph office, they stepped inside. The clerk yawned as they came in, then a strange look crossed his face. Steve wondered why, a slight sinking sensation hitting his belly for no reason he could pinpoint.

The operator frowned and set two telegrams atop the counter, waited.

190

Steve wrote out his new telegram before reading them.

While the operator tapped away at the key, Steve gathered up the telegrams and Sarah stood close by, watching him. The first confirmed what he expected: the gang's last known location, Deadeye. He set it aside and read the other.

REGRET TO INFORM MISS ELANA LIBERTY PASSED AWAY ON SEPTEMBER 24 FROM PNEUMONIA STOP YOUR PRESENCE REQUESTED BUT WERE UNABLE TO LOCATE STOP —

He needed to read no further. The telegram had been sent by Elana's father.

The sinking sensation in his belly hit home. He trembled suddenly, shaking his head in denial. 'Nooo . . . ' he whispered, a tear leaking from his eye. 'It can't be . . . '

'What is wrong, Steve?' Sarah touched his arm and he jerked away. Anger, disbelief and sorrow flashed across his face. A great welling pain in his heart. Dead? No, there had to be some mistake. Elana couldn't be dead, she was young, healthy, waiting for him in Matadero. Alive. Elana was alive. In a burst of fury he crumpled the telegram and hurled it to the floor. He stormed from the office, slamming the door behind him.

Sarah picked up the piece of crumpled paper and opened it. After reading the message, she glanced at the operator, who looked pained.

'I'm sorry, ma'am,' he said. She nodded, then left the office, going after Steve.

Steve didn't stop walking until he reached the end of the boardwalk. He stepped off into the dust, shaking, dazed, a cascade of emotions overtaking him.

She can't be gone!

The words thundered in his mind, a lie. He shook his head, tears running from his eyes and tracking down his face. '*Nooo!*' he shouted at the sky. He slammed his fists into the wall of a building until blood ran between his fingers.

She couldn't be gone, she couldn't be gone, she couldn't be —

Gone.

Flashes of memories taunted his mind. Joy, sorrow, happiness, hurt. Her face, her lovely face. A cloud of blonde hair and sparkling eyes. He saw her dance before his mind, waltzing at the church social with him, felt her warmth as he held her in his arms, felt her heart beating, low, gently, beating next to his, beating for all eternity.

Beating no more.

She was dead.

Gone from him. And no power on earth could change it.

I have come to say goodbye . . .

He knew. He knew with the force of a thousand screams why he had felt so apprehensive last night, knew why the great black bird of death had visited his dream, knew why she had told him she had come to say goodbye. Some unknown power had granted him her presence one last time.

Goodbye.

With uncontrollable bitterness he suddenly despised the sound of that word. He knew he always would.

He collapsed to the ground, sobs racking his body, tears seeping into the dust. He pounded his fists against the hardpacked ground and prayed he could die and be with her, hold her again. But grief was never a merciful executioner. It was a mocking warden.

He didn't know how long he stayed that way. It felt like hours but he knew it was only moments before a gentle hand touched his shoulder. He looked up, tears and dirt streaked on his face. Sarah. Through blurred vision he saw the sorrow of death reflected in her eyes and knew she, better than anyone, understood.

She knelt beside him and eased an arm beneath his. She held him in the morning light, trying to comfort him and a sudden hollowness swelled inside him, an emptiness that told him he was utterly and completely alone.

'I am sorry . . . ' Sarah whispered. 'So sorry.'

'She's gone . . . ' was all he could say and the words hurt more than any wound delivered by bullet or arrow.

'I know.' She held him tighter.

'I saw . . . the bird of death in my nightmares. I ignored it. I should have gone back.'

'You could have done nothing, Steve. It was not within your power.'

'I could have been there! I could have held her!' He suddenly pulled away from her, bolting to his feet and staggering away. She started after him, but he turned, the look in his eyes stopping her. He needed to be alone.

Alone.

He would have that now. Perhaps he would have it forever.

Night swallowed Deadeye and Steve Matthews felt as if his life had trickled away with the sunlight. Hours passed in a blur, filled with aching hurt and bitter-sweet pain. He hadn't returned to the deputy's office; he had merely wandered in the woods at the outskirts of town, waves of grief rushing through him so intensely he would collapse to his knees and sob. Grief intermixed with perversely elative moments where he recollected her, the little things she used to do; smiles and tears of joy, early morning horse rides and nights spent walking along the creek, katydids chirping, water murmuring. The day he'd asked her to marry him ran through his mind, poignant as the first bite into a sour peach. At times he caught himself laughing with uncontrollable emotion, almost hysterical.

He spotted the crow once, eyeing him from a branch, and he shouted at the bird, 'Get away from me, you sonofabitch! Haven't you done enough?' The bird took flight in a harsh flutter of wings and damning screech, leaving him alone.

Alone.

Sarah was right; he knew that. It would have made damn little difference had he been there, though surely her father would see it different. He would blame Steve for accepting a job that took him so far from home so near the wedding. The elder Liberty hated the business of manhunting, glorified murder, in his opinion, no place for any son-in-law of his. He had objected to the courtship from the beginning, threatening to not allow the marriage until Elana convinced him Steve would quit the business and settle down after the wedding.

She would have died whether you were by her bedside or out in the wildernesses.

He told himself that over and over. He had not the power to prevent it; the most powerful Apache shaman could not have halted the bird of death's fateful swoop.

I could have held her . . .

Yes, that much he could have done. He could have kissed her dying lips, told her goodbye. He could have at least done that.

Instead he was here, hunting a man whose face he'd never seen, an outlaw gang he shouldn't have cared less about. Let some other lawman bring them down. What business was it of his?

None. None of his goddamned concern.

Something had changed inside him. He felt it, like a bitter winter wind. Something had grown dark, malevolent, vengeful. He no longer saw the West in the same fashion, for now it was an empty cruel place, bleak and arid, a desert of wasted emotions, gleaming like bones, stinging like scorpions; a place bequeathed to the likes of the Widow Gang and their ilk. *They* belonged here. Not him. They belonged here to cause suffering and pain. Folks like him and Sarah, they just lost what was theirs, what they loved. A pity. A goddamn pity. So much beauty in a world where death held sway. Death and loneliness.

Dazed, Steve finally stumbled his way back into town as dusk bruised the landscape. Staggering into the saloon, he bought a bottle of whiskey from the dove who ran the place and sat himself at a corner table, giving only quick acknowledgment to the aftermath of the Widow Gang's assault — bullet holes and broken mirrors, tables with holes punched through their tops, bloodstains in sawdust. He paid it no mind. He didn't give a damn about gang or anything else except his pain, and he'd damn well drown in it for the time being.

He gulped from the bottle, letting the liquor burn its way down his gullet. It did little to ease the coldness inside him, the aching sorrow. If anything, he felt more maudlin, slightly whoozy.

The batwings creaked and he looked up. Sarah stepped into the saloon and slowly came over to his table, looking at him with that damnable pity in her eyes. He downed another slug of whiskey and wished she would leave him be. Wished she would stay.

'May I sit?' She indicated a chair beside him.

'Suit yourself,' he said with no particular emotion.

'When Jason died, I felt as you do.' She bowed her head, looked back up. 'I felt my heart wither and all happiness leave me like winter flowers. I despised the outlaw for murdering him, despised him with all my dead heart. I still do.'

Steve let out a mocking laugh. 'Well, I ain't got no one to hate, Sarah. No one but myself.'

'You are wrong. You cannot blame yourself for circumstance.'

'Can't I?' He took another swig of

whiskey, feeling the lightness in his head increase. Damned if he couldn't blame himself. Damned if he wasn't doing a right good job of it.

Her hand slid over his forearm and he had the urge to pull away, yet at the same time wanted to hold her, feel her warmth and comfort, let her take some of the God-awful hurt from his heart.

'She loved you, Steve. She loved you and would not want you to blame yourself.'

He gazed at her, eyes flooding, though he would not let the tears flow. The heaviness in his soul deepened. 'If I had married her earlier, given this up — '

'It would have made no difference. She grew ill. You do not hold the power of life and death.'

'You're wrong, Sarah, 'cause that's just what I hold. I take life, and I can grant it as easily. That's my job.'

'For the guilty, but not for other

men and not for her. I could no more have stopped that outlaw from killing Jason than you could have stopped her illness.'

Some of the dullness left his eyes and he stared into hers, seeing the gentleness there, the empathy. 'But tomorrow that man will die, Sarah, and you'll have that satisfaction.'

'Beyond that I will have what you have. The loneliness that haunts my dreams, the ghost of his kindness and good deeds and the whisper of his touch when I reach out for him in the dark.'

A sudden wave of pain brought a fresh round of tears to his eyes. Sarah's eyes grew moist as well. She felt what he felt and that would forever join them.

She drew him close, holding him as the moments dragged by. In her arms he felt comfort and for the moment that was enough.

★ ★ ★

When dawn streaked dusty pewter light through the barred windows, Steve was still sitting on his bunk, back pressed to the stone wall, mind lost in the past. He hadn't slept the entire night and though he knew that would do him little good for the task that lay ahead, he couldn't have changed it had he tried. There was no sleeping and whether he met death at the hands of the outlaws was of little concern to him. The cards would fall where they may. It was all bastard fate, anyway. If he'd learned one thing from Elana's death, he had learned that. He would protect Sarah with his life, see to it her man was avenged, but that was all. After that . . .

After that he would deal with his loss, his grief. For now the job at hand would give him a brief and welcome respite from the pain.

He stood, then poured himself a cup of coffee, watching as the deputy busied himself with last minute details, then headed out to collect the man he'd enlisted to join the posse. Steve cast Sarah a glance and she looked at him with hollow eyes circled with darkness. She hadn't slept either. She sat on her bunk with her arms folded around her knees.

The door rattled open and he looked over to see the deputy enter with another fellow.

'It's time,' said the deputy, face slightly pinched. The other fellow's eyes held worry but resolve as he looked at Steve and Sarah. He was a local blacksmith named Harry Barter, husky and well muscled, with a face wide and honest.

Steve nodded then checked the loads of his Winchester, which he passed to Sarah, and Peacemaker. This once, he almost relished the thought of killing a man. It gave him focus, direction. Whatever had changed inside him, the Widow Maker would pay for it. In spades.

They stepped out into the bright morning sunshine that belied the seriousness of their mission. Climbing into their saddles, they rode in silence, each man — and woman — grim-faced, and cantered on the deadly task ahead. Bringing down the Widow Gang would be no cakewalk. Any one of them stood high chance of not making it back alive. The thought was sobering as thunder in the Rockies.

The sun climbed higher, splashing sugar and honey over the land. The tranquil beauty of the morning was subtly lulling, yet despite that beauty, a pall hung in the air. It seemed as if the birds had stopped singing and the fragrance of autumn had turned stale. As if the beauty was merely an illusion and the day had been sapped of its vitality, its life.

Time flowed like grief and snatches or memory, glimpses of Elana's face, invaded unguarded moments. He felt tears well but forced them down. He noticed Sarah looking at him occasionally, sorrow and concern blatant in her eyes. He saw pain naked in her eyes as well. Today something would end for both or them and neither dared look at what lay beyond that.

Three hours later they reached the area the deputy had marked out on his map. The stream twisted though the rugged woodland a few hundred feet down to the left and the land rose in uneven bounds to the right. Scattered boulders and stunted trees, jagged brush and depressions ample enough to hide a man, spotted the hillside. Reining up, they dismounted and tethered the horses out of sight to cottonwood branches. Within moments they selected the positions the deputy had plotted on the map and hunkered down. The wait was nerve-jangling, tedious. Each cast occasional looks at the others, but few words passed between them.

The sun edged higher into the crystal sky. An eagle glided overhead and Steve wondered where the damn crow had gotten off to.

A distant sound riveted his attention

and he looked over to see the deputy
had caught it as well.

Hoofbeats.

The stage was due any minute, but
these sounds came from far left. The
outlaws! A splashing. They were fording
the stream. He nodded to the deputy,
whose lips tightened into a pale line.

It was time. The deputy's assumption
had been on the mark. The gang was
approaching and within moments the
stage would come from the south.
He heard a distant rumble even as
the thought crystallised in his mind.
His heart quickened. Beads of sweat
broke on his forehead. He set himself
and watched intently, finally spotting
movement.

The outlaws slowed as they approached,
cautious. Three of them angled left,
three right. Last time, the deputy had
informed Steve, they had boogered the
horses and caused the stage to crash.
He wondered if they would try the
same tactic again.

From the south the clamor of the

approaching stage grew louder. He heard hooves, the clatter of iron tyres.

He shot a glance at Sarah, mouthing a silent prayer she wouldn't be hurt. Her eyes were focused straight ahead, on the outlaws.

His gaze shifted to the stage. Two men poised in the driver's seat and he knew two guns waited inside. These men were fully prepared for the attack, expecting trouble. And they would meet it with fire-power and deadly intent.

The stage slowed. The drivers weren't taking any chances on repeating the first stage's folly. Steve wondered if it would alert the bandits.

The stage slowed to a crawl, stopped. Steve saw the two guns climb out, begin checking a wheel. So that was their ploy. Good. They would act like something was wrong, making themselves a supposedly easy target, and it would look perfectly natural. The gang would go for that and there would be no crash this time. The drivers climbed down, attempting

208

to appear casual, but throwing furtive glances to their right and left.

The ploy worked. The outlaws suddenly spurted ahead, coming from the left and from the right, endeavoring to get around to either side of the stage. Guns blazed, spits of flame snapping out, reports sharp and crisp in the autumn air. Bullets peltered the stage, burrowed into the ground, clinked from iron tyres. The horses reared, panicked, jangling their riggings.

The hired guns and drivers returned fire instantly; the air clouded with acrid blue smoke and whining lead.

The deputy and blacksmith bolted into action a beat behind the rest and Steve, crouching, triggered his Peacemaker. Ten feet away, Sarah levered shells into the chamber of her Winchester, blasting away. Her features remained emotionless but intense, purposeful.

The outlaws knew they were being attacked from different directions, now. Bullets whined around Steve. Slugs tore up the ground, gouging chunks of dirt and chipping slivers from boulders. Staccato gunfire flowed into a steady indistinguishable stream of reports. The air was blistered with hellfire and lead demons searching for lost souls.

A guard went down, clutching at his chest! He writhed, blood pumping out, splashing the dirt.

The outlaws leaped from their horses, skittering for shelter behind brush and boles.

The deputy scooted from cover, aiming for a large boulder closer to the action. A slug tore into his arm and kicked him off his feet. He rolled down the slope, managing to keep hold of his rifle.

The outlaws centred most of their assault on the stage. One of the guns suddenly stumbled backward. A gout of blood spurted from his mouth and he dropped his weapon, clutching at his throat and making choking sounds. A bullet had shattered his windpipe and Steve knew he'd be dead by the time he hit the ground.

Sarah aimed a volley of shots at the leader, who made himself an elusive target. The intensity in her gaze grew icy, driven by dread loss and frozen vengeance.

The deputy gained his feet but made himself too good a target as he sought the shelter of a huge oak. One of the outlaws sprang from behind a patch of brush and took aim.

The blacksmith leaped from his hollow and sought to fire on her, but she caught the glint of sun on steel and whipped her gun around, snapping a shot. He went down, lay still.

All qualms about shooting a woman suddenly vanished. Steve hastily triggered his Peacemaker; the outlaw girl did a double-step backward, a bullet slamming into her gut. She screeched and crumpled, crawling on her belly towards her horse.

The deputy reached the oak, gasping, blood streaming down his arm.

Steve didn't care for the way things were going. The deputy, blacksmith, a guard and gun were down, two of them permanently in all likelihood. But while the other guard and gun held their own and Steve and Sarah were in reasonably good positions, only one outlaw had been hit. The gang, taking no chances, were obviously experts at avoiding lead.

The wounded outlaw reached her horse, struggled to pull herself into the saddle. A guard sought to fire on her, but the outlaw leader triggered a shot as he scurried for his horse that caught the man in the face. With a spray of scarlet and a grisly scream the man hit the ground face first.

Sarah triggered three quick shots, all of them nipping at the leader's bootheels. He got behind a cottonwood unscathed and Steve heard Sarah let out a curse.

The lone hired gun blasted a shot that stopped one of the outlaw women in her tracks as she rose to fire on him.

Crimson exploded across her chest and she crumpled.

Three outlaws, as well as the leader, remained. The odds were swinging in the posse's favor. With the hired gun, Steve and Sarah it was three against four. The wounded girl had dropped her gun and was in no condition to fight. If the deputy could fire the odds went one better.

The shooting stopped. It was abrupt, the silence startling. Steve wondered for an instant what was happening. Then he knew. The gang had given up the fight! They were counting their losses and leaving the gold behind. Steve's mouth dropped open and Sarah shot him a questioning glance.

As the gang bolted for their horses, Steve and Sarah threw off their surprise and resumed firing, as did the hired gun. The deputy managed to get off a couple of shots but, poorly aimed, they went well wide of the mark.

One of Sarah's bullets skimmed another gang member across the shoulders and the outlaw girl stumbled in her step but still managed to reach her horse. Once they made their saddles they proved impossible to hit. Trees blocked the way and the outlaws leaned low, keeping behind as much horse flesh as possible.

Bullets ricocheted dangerously close to Steve and Sarah and they were forced to withdraw.

Hoofbeats. Retreating. Fading. The outlaws arrowed south, firing until the distance grew too great.

They had escaped, not without loss, but that fact did little to ease Steve's disgust. They had come so close to finishing the gang only to fail in the end. With the leader alive, the gang would rebuild, strike renewed terror into the West.

Steve let out a long sigh and rose, making his way down the slope. Sarah followed. He knelt beside the blacksmith; the man drew shallow rattly breaths. The bullet had punctured a lung. Steve doubted he would make it. The deputy came up to him, clutching his wound, which wasn't life threatening, but would need attention. They saw the gun examining the rest; he looked over with a slow shake of his head.

'Hell of a mess!' the gun snapped with disgust. 'Goddamn hell of a mess!'

'Didn't turn out the way I hoped,' said the deputy, face pinched.

Steve looked grim and eyed the south trail. 'They're headin' south. They got two wounded, at least one seriously. They shouldn't be too hard to catch up with.'

The deputy shook his head. 'I can't do it, Mr Matthews. I got three dead men and one on the way.' He nodded to the blacksmith. 'Need a sawbones myself — they hit my shootin' arm.'

Defeat washed across Steve's face. They went to the body of the outlaw girl, turning her over. Her mannish features were twisted in a grimace and her eyes glared defiant and damning even in death.

'Ugly critter,' the gun said, and spat at the dead girl.

In grim silence, they loaded the dead men into the stage, hoisted the blacksmith into a seat and tied his horse behind. The gun would take the reins, while the deputy rode beside them. They would reach Deadeye by nightfall.

'You ridin' back?' the deputy asked and Steve shook his head.

'Closest town's three days away and they'll be slowed. I'm goin' after them.'

A distressed look crossed the deputy's features. 'Only one of 'em's hurt bad. That still leaves three gals and the leader in good shape. Four against one ain't good odds, Mr Matthews.'

''Cept they won't expect me to come after them — '

'And it'll be four against two,' cut in Sarah, voice cold, unswayable. Her eyes locked on her Winchester. Steve wouldn't even try to argue with her.

The deputy shook his head. 'You've got a death wish, Mr Matthews, surely you do.' His gaze shifted to Sarah. 'Both of you.'

Steve turned and focused on the trail leading south, wondering if the deputy just might be right.

9

BRACE CARRIGAN signaled for his gang to hold up after they had ridden half a day. The sun was dipping into the slate-colored mountains and skeletal shadows stretched from trees. The air turned brisk. The outlaw didn't like the way things had turned out one damn bit. The strange feeling of doom stalking him felt stronger, now, as if some mythical devil had come a'calling. He spat, lips tightening into an angry line.

His first inkling of something wrong had come when he spotted the glint of sunlight off metal. That had told him there were men nestled among the boulders and brush; it had probably saved them from being wiped out completely. Still they had suffered more losses than expected: Bertha was dead, and Shale, well, Shale was in a bad way. He could hear her labored breathing as she slumped in her saddle. She'd barely maintained the pace set by him, which wasn't nearly half the speed he usually set after a job. Annie had taken a bullet, too, but her wound appeared superficial, merely a graze across the back of the shoulders.

He clenched a fist, thumping the saddlehorn. Goddamn, what the devil was going on? Irritation pricked him and he felt the urge to shudder for the first time in years. It was as if some creeping darkness had fallen over them ever since he killed that doc. Maybe that Chinagirl had cursed them. He heard them slant-eyes had a way of doing that.

Foolishness! Foolishness, plain and simple. But something was wrong; he couldn't deny that.

He pondered the ambush, wondering exactly who had attacked them. He got a clear look at the guards — they were unknown to him, but had definitely expected the attack. He admitted his mistake there, not in hitting the stage again, but in having the overconfidence to think no one would figure it out and try to stop him. No man had ever taken the notion to come after the gang before, so how could he be expected to figure it?

Of the others, he recognised the deputy from Deadeye. The fella had balls, he'd give him that. There had been three others, two men he'd never seen, but the woman . . . yes, that's what had made him decide to retreat. The Chinagirl. The doc's wife. Seeing her brought the feeling of doom home. Had they stayed they might have all died; he felt sure of it. That Chinagirl was bent on getting even; that warranted some caution, made her dangerous as a roused rattler. She had no regard for her own life and Brace lived by a code he would never break: he would kill menfolk aplenty, but never a woman. That put him and his gang at a disadvantage. While women had been killed occasionally in their robberies, it had never been by him. Bertha had always been a little loose with her gun, as had Shale on occasion. Always in the heat of battle, never intentionally, least that's what they told him. He could not shoot the Chinawoman, but she could shoot him.

He gave brief thought to who the other men were. One, the one he was sure had been vitally hit, looked to be a local who had joined up with the posse, but the other . . . the other had the look of a manhunter about him. Though Brace only caught glimpses of the *hombre*, he recognised that look, one he'd seen a hundred times — the look of a professional killer. He didn't like it. Anyone foolish enough to come after the Widow Gang had sand — or stupidity — and that made him as dangerous as the Chinagirl.

What would the posse do next?

Brace contemplated it. Would they head back to town? That was likely for the deputy and the gun. The lawman was wounded, had bodies to attend to. Hired guns were fickle; he'd likely signed on to ride with the stage, protect it, nothing more. He would go back to town and count his losses.

But the manhunter and the girl. If he reckoned right, they would track him. The manhunter had come on his own, had likely joined up with the law as a matter of convenience. And the Chinagirl was driven by vengeance; she had come this far to get even with him for killing her man and she would track him to the ends of the earth before giving up. Both knew Brace and his gang would be slowed by Shale. Brace eyed the back trail, feeling them dogging him, feeling it in his blood.

Brace's gaze swung to the trail ahead. The girls had formed a half-circle around him, awaiting orders. He glanced at Shale, who gasped rattly breaths. Blood streamed down her saddle. He shook his head and climbed from the saddle, indicating for the girls to do the same. April and May helped Shale down, setting her against a cottonwood. April soaked a bandanna with stream water and daubed the injured woman's face. Brace studied Shale intently.

'Start diggin' a grave,' he said in a low voice to May and Calamity Annie.

'Ain't that a bit premature?' Calamity asked, surprise on her gaunt face.

He shook his head sombrely. 'She's done for. Just a matter of moments.'

The outlaw leader went to Shale and knelt beside her. She tried to look at him, eyes half open, a weak smile on her lips.

'Let you . . . down, Brace . . . ' she said, words languid, strained.

He sighed. 'Hell, you did. We just ran into a bit of trouble, is all.'

Shale gave a thin toothless smile and her head suddenly dropped sideways. Her eyelids fluttered, stilled, and she stared sightlessly ahead, eyes empty. If he were a righteous man he would have said a prayer. But he wasn't and instead he merely closed her eyelids and nodded.

Brace stood, turning to the other women, April, May and Annie. In the past weeks he'd lost half his gang; the fact infuriated him. Feeling of doom or no he was not about to take that lying down.

'Bury her,' he ordered and the girls nodded, setting about the task. Brace stared off at the stream, lost in a cloud of anger and dark thought. When he turned back to them, he had made a decision.

'We best be goin'.' He moved towards his horse. Stepping into the saddle, he waited for the girls to mount. All three looked sombre and short-tempered.

'You think anyone will follow, Brace?' asked Calamity Annie, pushing up her spectacles.

Brace nodded. 'Reckon. One of them was a man-hunter, I'm right sure of it. He'll be an our trail. And that Chinagirl, she'll be with him.'

'You reckon we should ambush them?'

He shook his head. 'We'll head south for the rest of the day. Tomorrow we'll start doubling back, one by one.'

'Back to Deadeye?' Annie's voice held surprise. 'You ain't serious, Brace? We got whupped there!'

'Did we?' A dark look clouded his face. 'I recognised the deputy from that town. He must have arranged that little party this mornin'. I ain't about to let that go. Town needs a lesson that the Widow Gang can't be messed with, otherwise every goddamn lawdog in the West'll take a notion to try it.' He paused, eyes shifting to the mound of dirt and cross made from two sticks bound together with rawhide. 'That manhunter will find the grave and think we're still goin' south. Let him think that. Carson's a three-day ride from here. When he gets there he'll know he was wrong and come back. We'll be waitin' on him after we take care of the town.'

Worry crossed Annie's face. 'Don't seem like such a good idea, Brace. We need time to recoup.'

The look he gave her cut off any further protest. She set her lips in a frown.

Brace gigged his horse forward. April and May shot a glance at each other, then, along with Annie, followed suit.

★ ★ ★

As dusk fell, Steve Matthews drew up, Sarah coming to a stop beside him. He peered at the winding trail ahead, knowing it would be dark shortly and there would be no use in going any further until dawn. After a night of no sleep and the gunfight he felt exhausted, saddle-weary. He felt sure it had taken its toll on Sarah as well. In their present condition, they would prove little match for the Widow Gang.

He stepped from the saddle and led his horse to a cottonwood, tethering to a branch. Sarah did the same.

226

He stretched and went to the stream, where he splashed water into his face and wiped off on his bandanna.

Standing, he breathed a heavy sigh. 'We'll camp here for the night.' Sarah nodded, remaining silent. He set about collecting scraps of wood for a fire while she gathered an armload of dry leaves. In a short time they had the fire blazing. He pulled a blue enameled coffee pot from his saddle-bag and filled it with stream water and Arbuckle beans. They chewed on hardtack biscuits and, sitting next to the fire, watched the night fall.

'He can't be that far ahead,' Steve said, breaking the silence. 'Maybe half a day or less, depending on that wounded girl.'

'Perhaps closer,' Sarah said, voice low.

'Why do you say that?' The same feeling plagued him, but he had passed it off as wishful thinking.

'I have seen the black bird. He flies north, only to return a short time later.'

Steve poked with a stick at the ground 'Reckon I can't put my faith in birds at this point.'

'Perhaps you should.'

'I'm Apache, but I'm white, too, and that makes me practical where tracking is concerned. He'd be a fool to delay. No reason for him not get as far from Deadeye as possible and count his losses. Hardcases are all the same.'

'Perhaps this one is different.'

'How do you figure?'

'I looked into his soul the day he killed Jason. I saw blackness there, but something else as well. He has lost something, a long time ago and it will never let him be. He will not let things be taken from him ever again.'

Steve sighed and shook his head. 'Still, he's left a clear trail. Have to go with that.' He went silent and lay back, resting his head on his saddle, staring up at the stars. Dark sorrow washed over him when he thought of Elana. Moments later, exhaustion claimed him and he fell into a disturbed slumber.

The black bird rose before him, fluttering until the beating of its wings crescendoed into an ominous crushing beat. With a screech, the bird exploded into fragments that swirled and fell back, forming into the image of Elana, dressed in a black gown. He reached for her, her name touching his lips, and she smiled.

'She needs you now, Steve. You need her . . . ' A whisper, dissolving into the hushing breeze.

He awoke with a start, a gasp escaping his lips. Tears streaked down his face and he put his head in his hands. Sarah, still awake, came to him and held him until he fell back to sleep.

When he awoke, he felt far from refreshed. Sunlight streamed through the canopy of fall leaves and boughs, warming his face. The fire was still burning low and Sarah had prepared another pot of coffee.

Hitting the trail within half an hour, Steve read sign along the way as expertly as any Apache scout. The gang had passed this way; of that there could be no doubt. He saw splotches of dried blood, a steady trail of it, and reckoned the wounded girl was not long for this world.

A little past ten, they came upon the grave.

Steve dismounted and Sarah stepped from her saddle. Going to the grave he knelt and stared a moment at the makeshift cross.

He peered at Sarah. 'Looks like that wounded gal didn't make it. Now they surely got no reason to go back. No need for a sawbones.' He stood, gaze scouring the area, picking out tracks that led south. The gang would make better time, now, and he wondered if they would skip the next town altogether, simply disappear into the landscape.

He climbed back into his saddle, waited for Sarah to mount, then looked at her.

'They'll be faster, now. We'll lose

a little time but we'd best stop in Carson even if they don't and form us a posse. This time I want to make sure he doesn't escape.'

The Chinese woman nodded and a sudden cawing drew his attention. The crow dived overhead, flying erratically, darting from branch to branch in a northerly pattern, letting out squawks. He cursed the bird inwardly, shaking his head and Sarah looked at him, but said nothing.

They moved on, Steve alert for any sign of a divergence in the outlaws' path. Sooner or later he expected them to fork south-west, avoid Carson and head towards Colorado or Utah.

With each passing mile an anxious feeling strengthened within him. The occasional cawing of the crow made his nerves tight. It continued to swoop from branch to branch, take flight, backward, forward. The vegetation grew thicker, more rocky, harder to read. He drew up, some deep sense of something amiss nagging at him.

'What is it?' Sarah asked.

The crow landed on a branch, took off north again.

He studied it a moment, then looked at the ground and climbed from his horse.

'Steve?' Sarah asked when he said nothing.

'Something's wrong, Sarah. I don't know what, but it is.' He scouted the area, going ahead on foot a short while. After careful examination of the vegetation and disturbed dust, he let out a grunt.

He turned to the Chinese woman. 'They've lost two horses, one with a rider, one empty, judging from the depressions of the hooves.'

Sarah looked puzzled. 'How is that possible?'

He shrugged and climbed back into the saddle, gigging his horse into motion. They rode another half-hour. The sun climbed higher and the day grew warm.

The outlaw leader suddenly stepped

on to the trail before him. Steve froze, a gasp escaping his lips. He'd never expected that; none of the signs had pointed to it. The move caught him completely off guard. His hand started for his Peacemaker, halted in mid-action.

Something was wrong. The outlaw made no move towards them; he just stood there, laughing. As suddenly, the Widow Maker dissolved when Steve blinked Elana stood there, now, dressed in the flowing back gown, arm raised, finger pointing backward along the trial.

'Elana . . . ' he whispered, disbelief flooding his mind. The images shook him and his head began to whirl. Suddenly Elana exploded into black fragments that fell back, forming into the huge black bird. With a thunder of beating wings, the creature flew straight for him. He ducked to avoid it, but it cut a path between him and Sarah and disappeared behind them. He twisted in the saddle and looked backwards, seeing only empty air.

In a tree the crow cawed and took flight northward.

When he turned back, Sarah was looking at him, worry in her eyes.

Steve hesitated, pondering the visions, coldness washing through him. Had he really seen the outlaw? Elana? The huge bird? Maybe he *was* going loco. Maybe grief and disappointment did that to a man. 'Did you see them?' he asked finally.

'I saw nothing.' Her eyes swept the trail ahead, the worry in them deepening. 'What did you see?'

Steve swallowed. 'This'll sound loco, but I saw . . . I saw the outlaw and Elana, on the trail.' He nudged his head towards the trail. 'The bird, too. It came right at us, then disappeared.'

'I saw no bird, except for the crow that guides you.'

Steve stared at the empty trail, confusion and vague fear taking him. He was exhausted, burdened with grief. Perhaps that explained the visions.

Perhaps it did not.

He could not deny the vision, had no explanation for it, but it left him with a nagging impression he was being alerted to something, something he felt in his Apache soul but was reluctant to believe.

There's something wrong . . .

What?

He climbed from the saddle and, kneeling, examined the trail where the vision of the outlaw appeared. The sign was immediately obvious. One horse, now. The other had slipped off left and entered the stream, coming out on the other side most likely, he reckoned. What did that mean? He went back to his horse and sat in his saddle for long moments, Sarah silent beside him.

'Where I saw the vision,' he said at last. 'There was sign the gang lost another horse. It crossed the stream.'

Surprise lighted in her dark eyes. 'What does it mean?'

Steve gave her a serious look, frowned. 'It means the Widow Maker is more on the ball than I gave him credit for. I let my grief get in the way of my tracking sense. The vision gave it back.' He straightened in the saddle, glancing backward. 'They're headin' back to Deadeye.'

The surprise in her eyes deepened. 'What?'

'They're headin' back. I should have guessed it when I first noticed horses splitting off. He sent the slowest girl first, the one leading the spare horse. Another crossed the stream and likely skirted it at a distance until she could swing back across on to the trail. Probably another went up the hills right. Reckon if we keep goin' the tracks will disappear completely.'

'Why would they return to Deadeye?'

'This outlaw ain't like no others. I should never have thought he was. Like you said, he won't let things be taken from him. My guess is Deadeye's gotta pay for his losses there and he'll kill the deputy as a lesson to others who might take a notion to follow him.

He knows we'll be followin' his trail to Carson and he knows damn well we'll figure out what happened by the time we get there. He wants to square things with us, too. He's just issued us an invitation.'

Sarah looked backward along the trail, gaze lifting to the sky. 'The bird was telling you that.'

Steve nodded and looked up, too, scanning the woodland for any sign of the crow, but the bird had vanished.

10

THE Widow Gang hit Deadeye in a flurry of beating hoofs and flying lead. The time had come for retribution.

Their horses skidded to a stop, reared, neighing and kicking up clouds of dust. Townsfolk, stricken looks on their faces, dashed for cover inside stores and homes. Two men fell under a hail of gunfire, slamming face first into the boardwalk; blood pooled on dusty wood, streamed over the side. Women shrieked and scurried into buildings, slamming doors, a few remaining beside their fallen husbands, screaming, crying.

The attack came swift, brutal, without mercy or restraint. Brace would give Deadeye no chance to retaliate. This time he would devastate the town before someone mounted any type of counter attack. And if that damn fool deputy had the notion he'd gotten away with what happened last time or yesterday, he was in for a deadly shock.

Brace emptied his Schofield and hastily reloaded, triggering shots at buildings and barrels. Troughs spouted arcing streams of water. Wood splintered from doorframes and window sills. Glass shattered with loud jangles. Around him the gals whooped and hollered, blasting away with gleeful abandon and raging bloodlust.

The door to the marshal's office burst open and the deputy, arm in a sling, stepped on to the boardwalk, shock and befuddlement on his face.

April and May fired on him in the same instant. The lawman never even had the chance to draw. He went down under a hail of lead, smashing into the boardwalk and rolling off into the street.

Rage boiled in Brace's veins and he sent another slug into the lawman's body for good measure.

I'll kill you, you bastard!

A fever took him, splashed with images of the day his father killed his mother. For an instant he couldn't separate present and past, but then the town reappeared before his vision, as the shouting and thunder of shots slowed. Dust wisped across the street, chased by blue gunsmoke. The trickle of water from leaking troughs reached his shot-stunned ears, the muffled sobs of new widows. Music to his ears. Devastation, perhaps enough for the moment, but not enough for the final tally. Brace smiled as an eerie silence descended on the town. Yes, Deadeye had only begun to answer for its sins.

A man scooted from the saloon and sent a bullet in their direction. A foolish, foolish man whom Brace instantly recognised as the hired gun from the stage. The outlaw's smile widened into a grin. He aimed and squeezed the trigger. The man stuttered in his step, bounded sideways and crashed into the wall of a building, crimson splashing his chest. He hit the ground, lay still.

Easy pickin's, Brace thought. Damn easy pickin's. The town had yet to recover from his first visit. He glanced at the shattered bodies, sobbing women. 'I'm doin' y'all a favor!' he yelled.

I'll kill you, you bastard!

Calamity Annie broke the silence. 'What now, Brace?' She leaned a forearm on the pommel.

'We wait.' His voice came like ice and his eyes narrowed. 'That manhunter will figure out he's been tricked and come back this way lookin' for us. We'll be waitin' on him. I don't want any loose ends.'

Annie's brow crinkled. 'What about the Chinagirl? She's gonna come with him.'

Brace thought it over. The Chinagirl was dangerous and she had a hankerin' to see him buried. She would hunt him to the ends of the earth. He couldn't risk that. But he had held to his code too long to break it now. Something inside wouldn't let him. But one of his gals . . . well, some things were out of his control, weren't they?

'She's dangerous . . . ' was all he said.

A thin smile turned Annie's lips.

★ ★ ★

Deadeye came into view as dusk dragged shadows from their hiding places and frosted the air. Steve felt dread knot in his belly as he peered at the town. Riding closer, his apprehension strengthened. Gloom hung over Deadeye, a deathly stillness. He gazed about, spotting holes in walls and troughs, shattered windows showing no light. Dark patches stained the boards and dust. A chill swept through him and he slowed.

Death had ridden through Deadeye.

And death was still here; he could feel it.

Sarah glanced at him, porcelain

features grim but determined. 'They have been here.'

He nodded. 'We can't be more than a few hours behind them.'

He guided his bay to the side and stepped from the saddle, eyes roving, alert for any sign of an ambush. If they were here, then where? Hiding? Waiting? He drew his Peacemaker as Sarah climbed from the saddle, bringing her Winchester.

Easing on to the boardwalk, he made his way down the street. The town appeared deserted, moribund. If the signs of damage were any indication, the Widow Maker had struck with cold, calculated fury. They had likely murdered a good many menfolk, though he saw no bodies. Steve's gaze took in every spot a man might hide, but he saw nothing, no movement, no sign of life. Deadeye might just as well have been a ghost-town.

Shadows swayed and a slight breeze stirred the dust in the street. The stillness felt menacing.

Where are they?

The question taunted him. The gang was here; he felt sure of it. But where? What were they waiting for? He threw a glance at Sarah, seeing the same questions on her face, along with worry.

As they reached the marshal's office, he eased the door inward and stepped inside. Sarah stifled a gasp and Steve tensed. The bodies of the deputy and hired gun lay on bunks in the cells, mocking them. Blood had pooled on the floor. Both stared sightlessly upward, ghastly expressions on their faces. A stench of an abattoir hung in the room.

Sarah's face bleached and her hands went to her bosom. 'Where are they?' she voiced, words almost a whisper.

Steve shook his head. 'Waiting, I reckon. Waiting for us to come to them. This is their callin' card, tellin' us they aim to repay old debts.'

He moved to the window and gazed

out into the street, searching for any hint of movement. He saw none.

Turning back to Sarah, he said, 'It'll be dark soon. The odds'll be better if they don't see us comin'.'

'Where will we find them?'

He shrugged. 'Reckon they won't make themselves too hard to locate. He knows we'll come to him. He thinks he's got all the time in the world, but he don't. He don't have no time.' Steve's eyes narrowed. A grim sense of finality moved through him. Before this night was over, Deadeye would witness more death. His only worry was for Sarah, her safety. Deep inside himself he wished circumstances had been different, for in the deathly gloom of the office he realized he had come to love the Chinese woman who had suffered through so much, strong and silent. He had no right to love her, not now, not with the shadow of Elana's death hanging over him and Sarah's own loss. But he did. He couldn't deny it. Life was funny that way sometimes, quirky and morbid in its humor. His gaze shifted to her and a frown touched his lips.

Sarah turned away, a strange look of remorse on her face. She remained silent.

'What's wrong?'

She looked back to him, a tear sliding down her cheek. 'Perhaps I was wrong, Steve.'

'About what?'

'About the Widow Maker.'

'What? I don't see as how. He killed your man, Sarah, and lots of others. He deserves to die.'

'He does, but perhaps my hate was wrong. Perhaps revenge is better left in the hands of the God above.'

'God won't smite this man, Sarah; He's asked me to do it, I'm convinced of that more than ever, now.'

'Are you? I am not so sure of anything any more.'

Steve shook his head. 'A little while ago you wanted to kill him so bad it scared me. What's changed?'

Her eyes locked with his and he saw raw emotion burning through the loneliness, the hurt. There was more than mere sadness and pain. Something deeper, unfathomable, something with a reborn spark of life.

'Perhaps I do not want you to die.'

Emotion swelled in his throat. He holstered his gun and went to her, holding her tightly as another tear strolled down her cheek. Then he looked into her eyes. 'I have to do this, Sarah. It's not my choice any more. That man won't just let us walk away. He won't take the risk that I'll follow him, try to ambush him again. He ain't the type who can live with ghosts around every corner. He'll make sure I'm dead before movin' on. But you should go. He don't kill women He might let you live.'

She shook her head, determination frozen in her eyes. 'No, I will go with you. If you must finish this, then I will stay by your side.'

Something deep inside overwhelmed

him and he kissed her lips gently, drawing her closer and holding her tight, her breath warm against his neck.

He forced himself to pull away. 'It's time,' he whispered. He moved to the door, stepped out on to the boardwalk. Night had claimed Deadeye and the street was pitch-black, except for one light that had not been on a moment ago. A beacon. A beckoning. A calling out.

'The saloon,' said Sarah, coming up behind him.

'He wants us to know where he is.'

Drawing his Peacemaker, he moved across the street, Sarah trailing him, a ghost in the darkness. He edged along the buildings towards the saloon, keeping his back to the wall. Reaching it, he kept Sarah behind him as he peered inside.

He saw two women, Mex girls, sitting on the edge of a table, holding guns on three bargirls who cowered on barstools. Three bodies lay sprawled on the floor, locals unlucky enough to be caught in the saloon when the gang rode in. Fresh blood soaked the sawdust in places.

The drawing back of a hammer stopped him cold. A chill trickled down his spine.

'Welcome home, manhunter,' a raspy voice sounded behind him.

Steve edged around to see a man standing in the shadows, a man with one eye and a Schofield trained on his chest. To his left stood a mousy-looking girl jamming a gun to Sarah's temple.

The outlaw leader took a step closer. 'I don't know you, boy. Why you doggin' me?'

Steve didn't answer and the man laughed, looked at Sarah. 'You, I know, Chinagirl. You should have left well enough alone. I did you a favor that day, killin' your man.'

Sarah glared, hate like skulls in her eyes. 'You are a bastard,' she said, spite in her voice.

'You ain't the first to notice.' He

249

waved his gun. 'Drop the Peacemaker, kick it inside.'

Steve complied, letting his gun clatter on the boardwalk and booting it into the saloon. Calamity Annie plucked the Winchester from Sarah's grip.

'In!' ordered Brace. Steve turned and, keeping his hand high, pushed through the batwings. Brace followed, Sarah, prodded by Annie's gun, behind them.

The Mex girls straightened and moved around the table, keeping their guns leveled on the doves. The bargirls looked terrified but Steve reckoned they would be the lucky ones. The Widow Maker wouldn't kill them. But would he kill Sarah? He wasn't sure, but didn't see how the leader could let her live. If he did, he would be in constant danger of her following, killing him.

Steve took a step forward and Brace ordered him to stop. His gaze took in the surroundings in a glance. Of the three dead men, two had guns resting in holsters at their hips, but were too far away; he'd never make it to them. Within steps, he would be gunned down. His own Peacemaker lay too far to the left to do him any good. Two of the tables before him held lanterns, flames turned high. Both were within reach, but could they do him any good?

It didn't matter. In another minute he would die anyway. Then Sarah in all likelihood. He chanced another step forward, angling closer to a table.

'Stop!' Brace snapped. 'Don't get no notions, manhunter. You just turn around. I want to see your face when you die.'

Steve moved. He leaped forward, hand sweeping for the closest lantern. Scooping it up, he sent it flying towards Annie, who tried to jump back, but couldn't quite get out of the way. The lantern shattered, splashing kerosene flame across the sawdust. Some of the flammable liquid soaked Annie's clothes and she shrieked as flames swarmed up her trousers and shirt.

She dropped the Winchester and gun, and slapped frantically at her front.

Brace, stunned by the move, recovered from his shock and aimed the Schofield.

Sarah lunged, letting out a yell and knocking his gun sideways. The shot blasted and the bullet dug into the floor.

Steve, already in motion, dived sideways before the Mex sisters could swing their guns towards him. The doves, who shrieked continuously, dived for cover. Steve landed ten feet away, grabbing a table and flipping it over, then jerking a gun from one of the dead men's holsters.

Aiming hastily, the sisters fired. A bullet ripped across his side. The wound was nothing serious, just a graze. The other missed him by inches, tearing splinters from the edge of the table. He straightened, fanning the hammer and praying the gun was loaded.

It was.

He sent three shots their way. One went wide, but two others found their marks. One of the sisters dropped instantly, a hole over her heart. The other, hit in the arm, lost her gun but snapped a bolas from her belt, whirling it.

A popping sound behind him made him start. He saw the second sister drop to the floor, a bullet hole in her head. He glanced backward to see one of the doves had plucked a derringer from her bodice and fired at the Mex girl. He nodded a thanks and she scurried behind the bar. The sister pitched forward, slamming into the sawdust, which blew up in a cloud and settled over her body.

Calamity Annie was having no luck getting the fire out. She shrieked and danced about, flames devouring her clothing. The scent of scorched flesh filled the saloon, putrid, foul. Flames spread hungrily across the dry floorboards, gobbling sawdust and rising thick black smoke.

Steve leaped forward, only to stop short, gun raised.

The outlaw leader held Sarah in front of his chest. An insane light jittered in his eye as he held the gun to her temple.

'Let her go!' Steve kept his gun raised. The leader had him in a hell of a position. He couldn't fire without hitting Sarah.

The Widow Maker didn't kill women . . .

Did he?

It was a hell of thing to bet a life on but Steve saw no choice. They'd both die anyway. He looked into the Chinese woman's dark eyes and she gave a thin nod, as if reading his thoughts.

He was out of time. Flames were quickly surrounding them, lapping at walls, snaking up the bar and tables. Smoke stung his eyes, burned in his lungs. Calamity Annie rolled and gyrated on the floor. Her skin was bubbled and blackened and her hair was gone.

Steve took a step forward. 'Let her

go!' he said again.

The outlaw peered at him, a strange light in his eye. 'No, Pa. You won't hurt her again. I won't let you!'

Steve hesitated, puzzlement on his face. 'What?'

The Widow Maker's cheek twitched. The look in his eye was distant, lost. 'Ain't gonna let you, Pa. You hurt her enough. It's my place to hurt things, don't you know that? — *I'll kill you, you bastard*!'

He flung Sarah away from him and swung his gun to Steve. The move caught Steve off guard and the outlaw fired before the manhunter could trigger a shot.

Steve dived but not in time. The slug punched into his shoulder, the same shoulder pierced by the arrow. He lost his gun; it twirled across the floor. He clutched at the wound, blood streaming between his fingers but he had no time to worry about it. He dove forward and left before the Widow Maker fired again.

He crashed into the outlaw, barely moving him. The leader arced a blow with the gunbutt, aiming for Steve's face. It connected, rattling his teeth and sending a spray of blood from his nose. Pain shocked his face and he knew his nose was broken. He crumpled to his knees, dazed, blood streaming down his face, off his chin.

The outlaw jammed the gun to Steve's forehead and Steve pressed his eyes shut. He was dead. In the next instant a bullet would crash through his brain and there was nothing he could do to stop it.

A sharp cry cracked above the roar of the flames.

Steve opened his eyes.

The outlaw swung his head.

Sarah put a hole in his forehead.

She had snatched up her Winchester, knowing the outlaw would kill Steve but would not fire on her. A fatal mistake.

The outlaw froze, a bullet in his head and shock on his features. He pitched backward, hitting the floor in a cloud of sawdust.

Sarah ran to Steve's side, helping him to his feet and guiding him from the saloon. The doves rushed out from behind the bar and dashed outside. In moments the flames roared up, sweeping through the saloon, surging through the batwings. The roof groaned and collapsed. Sparks sprinkled the night sky and thick black smoke billowed into the night.

Steve fell into Sarah's arms, bruised and battered but alive. But that mattered little compared to the relief that flooded him because Sarah had survived, unhurt, except for the scars the Widow Maker would leave on her soul.

'He's dead, Steve,' she whispered. 'I'm alone, now.'

'We're alone together.' The marbled glow of fire and shadows bathed their bodies as they stood holding each other in the street for a very long time.

★ ★ ★

Three months had passed since the downfall of the Widow Maker. Steve's shoulder and nose had healed under the careful ministrations of Sarah. After the news hit the papers, he had been hailed a hero, an iron-nerved, ice-blooded manhunter who ranked with the best, even rivaling folks such as Duel Winston and David Brenner.

But Steve wanted none of the glory. He saw no point in it because too much death had come from the events. He was no longer the starry-eyed manhunter who rode with a prayer and a mission. Something had changed inside him and it would stay changed. He'd been touched by darkness, the evil of men, the blood that soaked the West. He wanted no part of tracking down men, now, killing them. Life was too short, too precious, and it was meant to be spent with those you loved, not doing your damnedest to get yourself killed.

With the reward money, he'd purchased a tract of land miles north of Deadeye, away from the carnage and memories, but nestled within the majestic untamed wonder that was Wyoming. Sarah gladly came with him and he found his feelings for her deepening with each passing day. At times, Elana's memory overtook him and he found himself in tears in the dark of the night, only to have Sarah hold him and say she understood. And she did. He wondered for a spell whether it was possible to love two women at once, and decided it was. Elana would want him to go on with his life, find happiness. With Sarah he found that, and she told him she loved him as well. They would marry by summer's end.

Steve had said goodbye to Sarah a week ago. He would return to her by the end of another, but first he would indulge the darkness inside him one more time before giving up his past life completely. He had reached Matadero just an hour ago, first guiding his horse to a small cemetery on the outskirts of town, where he had paid his last respects to Elana and wept.

After, he headed into town. As he rode through the main street, a feeling of chilled emptiness at what he had to do came over him. He reined up in front of the jail, hand sliding over the Peacemaker at his hip. Climbing from his horse, he pulled another gun from his saddle-bag and checked the load, making sure it was full and functioning.

He entered the sheriff's office and a thin man looked up at him from behind a desk.

'Steve, didn't know you was back,' the man said, though curiosity entered his eyes at the sight of the gun in Steve's hand and the other at his hip.

'Sheriff ain't here?'

'Nah. Went out of town for a week with his wife and that Indian deputy and left me in charge.'

'Got me a telegram from a Ranger

friend, said you still got Gonzales in jail . . . '

The man nodded. 'Got him back, you mean. He escaped a few months back, but didn't get too far. Caught him in a saloon in El Paso and hauled his sorry ass right back here.'

'He had friends . . . ' Steve explained how the hard-case had hired men to kill him and make it look like an Indian attack, and how Sarah had lost her home and all her belongings. As the deputy listened, his face went pale.

'Judas Priest, Steve!' he blurted when the man-hunter finished.

'I'd like few minutes alone with him.' A steely grimness narrowed Steve's eyes and the deputy eyed him with a certain chilled suspicion.

'Ain't regular, Steve. You know that.' He paused, running a finger over his upper lip. 'Ain't right to kill a man in jail.'

'He'll have his chance. You got my word on it. He wins, you make sure he never gets out again. I win, you won't have to worry about it. The sheriff's an ex-manhunter. He'll know the code we live by and I'll explain the details to him.'

'Steve . . . ' The deputy saw protesting was useless and reluctantly handed Steve a ring of keys. Steve nodded, and went through a metal door that led to the cells. The place had been recently expanded, but most of the cells were empty.

Except for one.

A man rested on a bunk in the third cell, a fore-arm draped over his eyes. Steve shut the door hard and the man lazily looked up, only to swing his feet suddenly off the bed when he saw who it was.

'Christ, you're alive!' the Mex said. 'What the hell you want?'

'You sent men to kill me, Gonzales, while you were out.'

'Prove it, *gringo*. I been here for months.'

'Don't need proof.' Steve stepped to the cell door and unlocked it, pushing it open. The Mex eyed him with suspicion and a small measure of fear.

'What the hell you bent on, *gringo*?'

Steve crouched and slid the gun across the floor. It stopped at Gonzales's feet. The Mex bandit stared at it.

'Pick it up,' ordered Steve, tone cold, controlled, hand poised over his own gun. 'You took something from a friend of mine. That makes it worse than tryin' to kill me. I might have let it go otherwise. But this gal didn't deserve any more loss in her life and you gave it to her.'

'What the hell you talkin' about?'

A dangerous smile traced Steve's lips. 'You don't have to understand it. Pick it up.' He nodded to the gun.

'No.' A sudden fearful defiance welded to the bandit's voice.

Their eyes met. 'Pick it up or I swear I'll shoot you where you sit.'

Silence. Strained, ominous. Their eyes remained locked and the Mex obviously saw Steve meant what he said.

The bandit moved suddenly, sweeping the gun from the floor and straightening, bringing it up.

Steve's hand slapped to his Peacemaker; the gun cleared leather in a blur.

A shot thundered in the confined area, deafening, final.

The Mex stared down at his shattered breastbone and the gun dropped from his numbed fingers. He looked up, horror on his face, then pitched forward, hitting the floor and going still.

Steve felt little sense of satisfaction. A job was done, that was all. Justice had been delivered and now he could walk away from it all. He wondered if it would haunt him.

He left the cell area, walking past the deputy, who stared at him with widened eyes and a bleached face.

'Last time I'll be seein' you, Steve?' he asked, voice strained. Steve nodded and went out into the street, climbing into his saddle and reining around. He could go back to Sarah, now, and the past would come to a close. A new life would begin. His soul felt heavy, but in time that would pass.

All things did.

As he rode slowly through the street he heard a cawing and noticed a crow alighting on the corner of a building, eyeing him. For the briefest of instants he wondered, then shook his head.

The world was full of crows.

THE END

Other titles in the Linford Western Library:

TOP HAND
Wade Everett

The Broken T was big. But no ranch is big enough to let a man hide from himself.

GUN WOLVES OF LOBO BASIN
Lee Floren

The Feud was a blood debt. When Smoke Talbot found the outlaws who gunned down his folks he aimed to nail their hide to the barn door.

SHOTGUN SHARKEY
Marshall Grover

The westbound coach carrying the indomitable Larry and Stretch headed for a shooting showdown.

FIGHTING RAMROD
Charles N. Heckelmann

Most men would have cut their losses, but Frazer counted the bullets in his guns and said he'd soak the range in blood before he'd give up another inch of what was his.

LONE GUN
Eric Allen

Smoke Blackbird had been away too long. The Lequires had seized the Blackbird farm, forcing the Indians and settlers off, and no one seemed willing to fight! He had to fight alone.

THE THIRD RIDER
Barry Cord

Mel Rawlins wasn't going to let anything stand in his way. His father was murdered, his two brothers gone. Now Mel rode for vengeance.

ARIZONA DRIFTERS
W. C. Tuttle

When drifting Dutton and Lonnie Steelman decide to become partners they find that they have a common enemy in the formidable Thurston brothers.

TOMBSTONE
Matt Braun

Wells Fargo paid Luke Starbuck to outgun the silver-thieving stagecoach gang at Tombstone. Before long Luke can see the only thing bearing fruit in this eldorado will be the gallows tree.

HIGH BORDER RIDERS
Lee Floren

Buckshot McKee and Tortilla Joe cut the trail of a border tough who was running Mexican beef into Texas. They stopped the smuggler in his tracks.

BRETT RANDALL, GAMBLER
E. B. Mann

Larry Day had the choice of running away from the law or of assuming a dead man's place. No matter what he decided he was bound to end up dead.

THE GUNSHARP
William R. Cox

The Eggerleys weren't very smart. They trained their sights on Will Carney and Arizona's biggest blood bath began.

THE DEPUTY OF SAN RIANO
Lawrence A. Keating and
Al. P. Nelson

When a man fell dead from his horse, Ed Grant was spotted riding away from the scene. The deputy sheriff rode out after him and came up against everything from gunfire to dynamite.

FARGO: MASSACRE RIVER
John Benteen

The ambushers up ahead had now blocked the road. Fargo's convoy was a jumble, a perfect target for the insurgents' weapons!

SUNDANCE: DEATH IN THE LAVA
John Benteen

The Modoc's captured the wagon train and its cargo of gold. But now the halfbreed they called Sundance was going after it . . .

HARSH RECKONING
Phil Ketchum

Five years of keeping himself alive in a brutal prison had made Brand tough and careless about who he gunned down . . .

FARGO: PANAMA GOLD
John Benteen

With foreign money behind him, Buckner was going to destroy the Panama Canal before it could be completed. Fargo's job was to stop Buckner.

FARGO: THE SHARPSHOOTERS
John Benteen

The Canfield clan, thirty strong were raising hell in Texas. Fargo was tough enough to hold his own against the whole clan.

PISTOL LAW
Paul Evan Lehman

Lance Jones came back to Mustang for just one thing — revenge! Revenge on the people who had him thrown in jail.

HELL RIDERS
Steve Mensing

Wade Walker's kid brother, Duane, was locked up in the Silver City jail facing a rope at dawn. Wade was a ruthless outlaw, but he was smart, and he had vowed to have his brother out of jail before morning!

DESERT OF THE DAMNED
Nelson Nye

The law was after him for the murder of a marshal — a murder he didn't commit. Breen was after him for revenge — and Breen wouldn't stop at anything . . . blackmail, a frameup . . . or murder.

DAY OF THE COMANCHEROS
Steven C. Lawrence

Their very name struck terror into men's hearts — the Comancheros, a savage army of cutthroats who swept across Texas, leaving behind a bloodstained trail of robbery and murder.

SUNDANCE: SILENT ENEMY
John Benteen

A lone crazed Cheyenne was on a personal war path. They needed to pit one man against one crazed Indian. That man was Sundance.

LASSITER
Jack Slade

Lassiter wasn't the kind of man to listen to reason. Cross him once and he'll hold a grudge for years to come — if he let you live that long.

LAST STAGE TO GOMORRAH
Barry Cord

Jeff Carter, tough ex-riverboat gambler, now had himself a horse ranch that kept him free from gunfights and card games. Until Sturvesant of Wells Fargo showed up.

McALLISTER
ON THE
COMANCHE CROSSING
Matt Chisholm

The Comanche, McAllister owes them a life — and the trail is soaked with the blood of the men who had tried to outrun them before.

QUICK-TRIGGER COUNTRY
Clem Colt

Turkey Red hooked up with Curly Bill Graham's outlaw crew. But wholesale murder was out of Turk's line, so when range war flared he bucked the whole border gang alone . . .

CAMPAIGNING
Jim Miller

Ambushed on the Santa Fe trail, Sean Callahan is saved by two Indian strangers. But there'll be more lead and arrows flying before the band join Kit Carson against the Comanches.

GUNSLINGER'S RANGE
Jackson Cole

Three escaped convicts are out for revenge. They won't rest until they put a bullet through the head of the dirty snake who locked them behind bars.

RUSTLER'S TRAIL
Lee Floren

Jim Carlin knew he would have to stand up and fight because he had staked his claim right in the middle of Big Ike Outland's best grass.

THE TRUTH ABOUT SNAKE RIDGE
Marshall Grover

The troubleshooters came to San Cristobal to help the needy. For Larry and Stretch the turmoil began with a brawl and then an ambush.

WOLF DOG RANGE
Lee Floren

Will Ardery would stop at nothing, unless something stopped him first — like a bullet from Pete Manly's gun.

DEVIL'S DINERO
Marshall Grover

Plagued by remorse, a rich old reprobate hired the Texas Troubleshooters to deliver a fortune in greenbacks to each of his victims.

GUNS OF FURY
Ernest Haycox

Dane Starr, alias Dan Smith, wanted to close the door on his past and hang up his guns, but people wouldn't let him.

DONOVAN
Elmer Kelton

Donovan was supposed to be dead. Uncle Joe Vickers had fired off both barrels of a shotgun into the vicious outlaw's face as he was escaping from jail. Now Uncle Joe had been shot — in just the same way.

CODE OF THE GUN
Gordon D. Shirreffs

MacLean came riding home, with saddle tramp written all over him, but sewn in his shirt-lining was an Arizona Ranger's star.

GAMBLER'S GUN LUCK
Brett Austen

Gamblers seldom live long. Parker was a hell of a gambler. It was his life — or his death . . .

ORPHAN'S PREFERRED
Jim Miller

Sean Callahan answers the call of the Pony Express and fights Indians and outlaws to get the mail through.

DAY OF THE BUZZARD
T. V. Olsen

All Val Penmark cared about was getting the men who killed his wife.

THE MANHUNTER
Gordon D. Shirreffs

Lee Kershaw knew that every Rurale in the territory was on the lookout for him. But the offer of $5,000 in gold to find five small pieces of leather was too good to turn down.

RIFLES ON THE RANGE
Lee Floren

Doc Mike and the farmer stood there alone between Smith and Watson. There was this moment of stillness, and then the roar would start. And somebody would die . . .

HARTIGAN
Marshall Grover

Hartigan had come to Cornerstone to die. He chose the time and the place, and Main Street became a battlefield.

SUNDANCE: OVERKILL
John Benteen

When a wealthy banker's daughter was kidnapped by the Cheyenne, he offered Sundance $10,000 to rescue the girl.

RIDE A LONE TRAIL
Gordon D. Shirreffs

The valley was about to explode into open range war. All it needed was the fuse and Ken Macklin was it.

HARD MAN WITH A GUN
Charles N. Heckelmann

After Bob Keegan lost the girl he loved and the ranch he had sweated blood to build, he had nothing left but his guts and his guns but he figured that was enough.

SUNDANCE: IRON MEN
Peter McCurtin

Sundance, assigned to save the railroad from a murder spree, soon came to realise that he'd have to fight fire with fire, bullets with bullets and death with death!